NO BOUNDARIES

PHOENIX, INC., BOOK 1

SE JAKES

1

THE 1967 MUSTANG SHELBY WAS A REAL FUCKING BEAUTY. COLE ran his hand over the bumper, focusing on her smooth lines that were goddamned perfection. But she was dirty—not garaged and in danger of being driven into the ground by the man who'd brought her in.

When he looked under the hood, he noted immediately that the mechanic who'd worked on her previously hadn't helped.

"Can you fix this?" the Mustang's owner asked.

Cole didn't catch his name, but it didn't matter. The guy was typical of the customers with high-end cars—monied, careless, collecting classic cars for the sake of collecting something—although he was younger and more handsome than a lot of the guys he dealt with. Not that it mattered to Cole—his concern was the car. "Yeah, not a problem."

"That's what the other mechanic told me last month. And the month before that." Mustang Man's voice had a slight edge to it.

Cole looked him in the eye. "They're not me."

Mustang Man's eyebrows shot up. It'd been a cocky thing for Cole to say, yeah, but he could damned well back it up. He had a gift for fixing cars and bikes. His youngest years had been spent in his father's garage, handing him tools, listening to him talk to the customers.

Those were the good memories.

There were so many bad ones that they tended to take over. Here, at least, he could mostly keep them at bay.

He continued examining the car, now that he had the Mustang Man's attention. Five minutes later, he finally looked up from the car to meet Mustang Man's gaze. "I'll let you know what I think it'll cost by tomorrow."

Mustang Man waved his hand. "Doesn't matter. I'll tell your boss that I'm authorizing any and all work, as long as it's done by the weekend."

Because it was Wednesday, with an entire garage flooded with cars to fix, so yeah, that was fair. Cole was definitely used to this type of owner—the world revolved around him and him alone. With the cash to back it up, Cole didn't doubt his boss at the garage would tell him to get this shit done and keep the customer happy.

Cole was, at times, too close to the memories of his other job for comfort. But he was truly a million miles from it. Well, several states, at least.

He leaned a hip against the car and stared at Mustang Man steadily. "I'll do my best to get it to you for the weekend. I'll check her out today and if it's going to take longer, I'll give you a call."

The guy nodded, then asked, "What about the weekend for *you*?" as his gaze raked up and down Cole's body, lingering between his legs and then sliding back up to his face.

It might've been flattering if the guy wasn't treating him like he was trying to purchase a service.

Cole motioned to the garage. "Lots of demanding customers —I'll be working straight through."

Mustang Man wasn't deterred. "I'll check back with you."

You do that, asshole.

Cole went toward the back of the garage to grab an intake form so he could start making a list of what the car needed, before going back to fixing the Porsche Boxster already on the lift.

He almost threw out the small piece of paper sitting on top of his workstation table— and since he kept it really neat, it stuck out. For a brief moment, before he saw what was written, he thought it might be Mustang Man's address or phone number or something. But the owner of the Mustang hadn't come back this way at all, and although Cole didn't recognize him, he'd gotten to the point where the men he'd fucked had become nameless and faceless. That's what made the job bearable to a lot of the guys—it had the opposite effect on him.

The note was written on heavy-stock paper—he realized this once he actually held it between his fingers. It was expensive but generic, with no imprint or initials. Elegant black ink sprawled across the page casually. It could've been an invite to lunch.

Instead, it bore something far more sinister.

Once a whore, always a whore. And I already paid. Now it's your turn.

No signature. Nothing to indicate who it'd come from, who'd come in and dropped his past back into his line of sight —into his future. But he didn't have time to freak because, at that moment, Jerry shoulder checked him.

Normally, Cole could see him coming a mile away, but the

note had shaken him. He shoved it into the pocket of his cargos and turned to face the sneering mechanic.

Jerry was maybe five years older than him and growing more and more resentful of the fact that Cole was increasing the garage's business with his skills. The boss had noticed—Cole had already gotten a raise, and shit like that got around fast. Most of the guys here were cool with him, but not Jerry.

Jerry had been calling him a faggot under his breath since the first week, when he'd shown Cole a naked female centerfold and Cole had told him she wasn't his type. When Jerry had pressured him, he'd finally told Jerry just what his type was. Obviously, Jerry couldn't seem to accept that.

He'd heard all Jerry's comments to the other mechanics, how he was worried that Cole was "after his ass".

Right. Because gay equaled wanting to fuck every single man that moved. "What the fuck, Jer?"

Jerry narrowed his eyes. "Why the fuck you collecting all the customers? You blowing them?"

"No, I let them blow me," he said, his stance relaxed and ready for Jerry to lunge at him. And Jerry didn't disappoint, head down like he was going to plow Cole over. Cole caught his arm, jerked it around his back and shoved him to the ground, more gently than Jerry deserved. Then he leaned down and said quietly, "Better be careful—this faggot's touching you... that's how we do the conversion."

"Get the fuck off me!" Jerry howled, and Cole let him go. He noted his boss coming out of his office, staring between the two of them, lifting his brows as if to say, *"Is this over?"*

"We're good, boss," Cole called to him. "Jerry tripped. I was helping him up."

Jerry had struggled to his feet and he nodded. The boss

went back up the stairs and closed his office, the rest of the guys went back to work and Jerry pointed at him. "Watch your back."

"Only if you watch mine," Cole told him and then walked away.

He'd just made it harder on himself—he knew that. A lot of the guys felt the way Jerry did, but they weren't as vocal. Hell, if he hadn't outed himself, the amount of guys who hit on him would've made him the butt of their joking anyway.

"Rough day?"

Cole turned around when he heard Styx's voice. Styx had been one of his first customers here at the shop—the guy was really tall—the kind of blond and blue-eyed handsome that people stopped to stare at. Now, Cole struggled to keep his voice casual when he said, "Same old."

But Styx's gaze leveled him. "Can I see the note that has you freaked the fuck out?"

Jesus, how long had Styx been here, watching him? He figured Styx'd seen the fight but... "Why?"

"Because you could use a friend."

Styx owned a PI business in town. So he was either a good guy or sniffing out potential customers.

Sometimes Cole hated being so cynical, but that's what'd kept him alive for this long.

Once a whore, always a whore. And I already paid. Now it's your turn.

Fuck. The edges of panic bled into his vision—he had to get Styx off his back. "The note's not important." He went to crumple it and throw it away, but Styx's hand was on his forearm. He stared up into Styx's haunted, kind eyes and said, "Get the fuck off me."

"Please, come sit down."

"I can't. I'm—"

"Going to pass out," Styx finished for him. There was no room left for argument, not when Styx was right. He let the man lead him to the nearest bench on the side of the garage, and he sat while Styx got him water. He realized he still had a death grip on the note as he tried to breathe evenly and hope the rest of the guys in the garage hadn't witnessed the whole damned breakdown.

"No one noticed," Styx assured him.

"Stop reading my mind." Cole heard the irritation in his own voice, but Styx ignored it and continued asking questions.

"Talk to me about the note."

"You're a customer," he told Styx hollowly, then downed the rest of the water.

"Ah, Cole." Styx's voice was resigned. "Come on. I've talked with you for a year."

"Business."

"Do you see me talking business with anyone else?"

No, Cole hadn't. He worked exclusively on Styx's, Law's and Paolo's cars and bikes. But still... "I don't want to tell you this."

"Why?"

"It's private. My life. You wouldn't understand."

"You have no idea what I'd understand."

"People say you and Law and Paolo," he started, then stopped because he had no idea why he'd blurted that out.

Styx smiled, and a light flashed in his eyes. Not an angry one, either. "People are right.

We're living and working together."

"You're *all*...together?"

"Oh yeah." His smile was wicked, and it made Cole laugh,

really laugh, for the first time in a while. "I think that's the first I've heard you laugh since I met you."

"It's been a long time." The note remained in his hand. He stared down at it.

"What's in the note?" Styx prompted again.

Cole looked up at him and finally admitted, "My past."

2

LAW

It was going to rain.

Law took four Advil out of the way of Styx's and Paolo's lines of sight. Of course they'd know, but they'd gotten better about asking him if he was in pain every five minutes. Most of the time he was cool with the coddling, but, like he told the men in his life, he knew when the weather was going to change before any of them. It was his body and all (although Styx would argue differently...and quite persuasively).

Now he raised his arms overhead to try to get some relief from the constant ache of too many childhood injuries and heard some cracking as he stretched.

His office was in the back of Phoenix, Inc.—Paolo and Styx were more the people persons. They didn't get a ton of walk-ins and the doors were locked, but they had staff and phones, and Law wasn't the best front man. His time alone, away from the noise, was his happy place...that was if he wasn't alone with Styx and Paolo, because they were his other happy place.

As soon as Styx came back from the garage, Law knew something was wrong. He wasn't any kind of psychic or anything, but he'd known there was something happening with Cole. He was actually surprised it took this long for Styx to figure out.

Cole was a lost boy—the way he and Styx and Damon had been. Paolo had been through hell, but a different kind of hell.

To some extent, they still thought of themselves as lost boys, called themselves such when they'd lived with Greg, the man who took them in, saved them from the streets and, to a much greater extent, from themselves.

Since then, Law and Styx had been able to spot them. They couldn't save all of them— and a lot didn't want to be saved— but they helped out at youth shelters and all the nurses at the local ERs had their phone numbers.

But seeing Cole...*fuck,* it was like seeing himself at twenty-something, fresh out of Delta training. Still fucked up then, trying to put his past to rest and unable to do so. When he looked at Cole, the pain came rushing back, and so he did his best to avoid the guy when forced to bring his bike into the garage. And he was sure Cole noticed, even though he tried to be as friendly as he could. Whenever he approached the garage, inevitably his gut would tighten and he would be right back in that place he didn't want to be. And Cole looked fine. He didn't ask to be rescued, and he didn't have that heavy look in his eyes like he was in complete danger. But he looked haunted, and Law knew that look too well.

Now, he heard Styx's voice boom through the office, "Marcus, you finish your case?"

"If you consider filing the paperwork as being done, then no," Marcus told him.

Law glanced out the door of his office and saw Styx wave his hand. "Got a job that's more important than paperwork. Meet me in my office in ten minutes."

Marcus nodded. "Got it, boss."

Ah fuck. It was *definitely* going to goddamned rain.

He moved to the meeting room in time to hear Paolo telling Styx, "I don't like paperwork either, but..."

"I'll do it for him," Styx said.

Law's hand tightened along the doorjamb and Paolo whistled under his breath. "This case hit a nerve."

"Yeah," Styx said quietly, and Law knew that tone. "It's Cole, the one who works at the garage down the street. He's in trouble."

"Knew it," he muttered from the doorway, and both Styx and Paolo turned to him. "Knew what?" Styx asked.

Law shrugged and moved to sit on the table. "Kid's haunted."

Paolo was closest to him, wrapped a hand around the back of Law's neck now and rubbed. Law practically purred under his touch. "Why didn't you say anything?"

"What's to say?" Law bent his head to keep encouraging Paolo's massage.

"That he needed friends," Paolo told him, now maneuvering so he could use both hands along Law's shoulders and back.

"He wasn't ready," Styx broke in, and Law raised his head a little to look at his old friend and lover. "And now he's in trouble."

"So why Marcus? Why not us?" Paolo asked, his fingers pressing the pressure points along Law's spine, making him groan out loud. He wondered if he could throw Paolo on the table and convince Styx to lock the door for a while...

Styx cleared his throat and wagged a finger at Law. Behind

him, Paolo snickered. "Can't blame me for thinking what I'm thinking—he's got good hands."

He was deflecting the Cole conversation—he knew that. And, dammit, they'd know it too.

"We'll help, but we're not what Cole needs. Not the most." Styx glanced through the open door and over at Marcus, who stood next to a desk, arms crossed, looking out the front window of Phoenix, Inc. The thousand-yard stare of a man who'd seen a lot of combat— maybe too much.

"And Marcus is what Cole needs? A cocky, arrogant asshole?" he asked, then paused. "Wait, I see your point."

Paolo snorted and Styx smiled. "Figured you would."

3

FOR STYX TO OFFER TO DO PAPERWORK, THIS CASE HAD TO BE important. Marcus had just put the most boring case in the world to bed. And for him these days, boring equaled good. Anytime someone wasn't shooting at him was a really good thing.

He'd worked for Phoenix, Inc. for nearly a year in an attempt to gain back his humanity. He owed Clint—Styx's old partner and Marcus's good friend—for that, for getting him out of the CIA, for leading him here to another group of guys who understood how reentry into the real world was a bitch.

The office mainly employed guys like him—former military or CIA—guys who could handle any situation, keep their mouths shut about the cases. Guys who needed to recharge, who needed a few wins under their belts, because no one won anything in the CIA. It was an endless loop of soul-sucking work that never seemed to make a difference.

Now, he saw Law and Paolo leaving the meeting room, and Styx leaned out and motioned for Marcus to come on in. He pocketed his phone and headed that way. Paolo smiled at him as he passed, while Law nodded stiffly, meeting his eyes for only the briefest of seconds—out of all of them, that guy was definitely the hardest to get to know.

Then again, that's what people said about Marcus. "So, you've got something for me— sounds pretty important," he said to Styx.

"It is." Without telling Marcus to sit—because he knew Marcus wouldn't—Styx leaned against the large, oval-shaped table and said, "New client's name's Cole—he works at the garage down the street."

Styx slid his phone in front of him. On the screen was a picture, obviously clicked without Cole's knowledge. Marcus stared at it for a long moment before dragging his eyes away. "He's young."

"Twenty-three," Styx confirmed.

Cole was his type—definitely his type, one he'd avoided for a hell of a long time. But Styx couldn't have known that, even though he seemed to know everything. And Cole was also a goddamned kid. Okay twenty-three wasn't exactly a kid, but to his thirty-four very battle-scarred years, twenty-three was light-years away from where he was. "So what's the deal?"

"Possible stalker."

"Any idea who?"

"I was there when he got this note—it's a direct threat." He put it in front of Marcus as well, gave him a chance to read the chilling words, then continued, "He says this is the first time that's happened. It's related to his past, but I didn't really press. He was pretty shaken."

"So you want me to get the details? Figure out if this is worth taking?"

Styx looked at him, his eyes cool and questioning. "It's

worth taking, Marcus. We're going to need more intel, but we need kid gloves on this."

Marcus snorted—he couldn't help it. "I think you picked the wrong guy."

"Thing is, I don't think so." Styx studied the picture on the phone again before clicking it off the screen. "He doesn't have the money to afford us, but we're doing it anyway."

Marcus didn't argue—it was Styx's dime, after all, and if he wanted to give away services, so be it. Still... "You know I'll question him. And he's not going to like it."

Styx hesitated for a moment before he nodded.

Marcus trusted Styx's gut—all of the guys who worked here were too damned good at what they did not to trust Styx's instincts as much as they did their own. But when a handsome young man tugged at the heartstrings, Marcus's suspicions reared their heads. And that's what Styx and the others hired him for.

"He's expecting you—he's done at six and I told him to wait for you at the diner right after," Styx told him.

"I'll be there." Marcus stood. "Any other cases?"

"Focus on Cole full time until you figure out who's sending him the notes and what we're doing about it."

True stalking cases weren't easy—in fact, they made for some of the toughest, most heartbreaking ones because getting an order of protection rarely helped. In fact, law enforcement couldn't do much until the stalker actually threatened the person physically, and by the time it got to that, it was typically too late. Businesses like Phoenix were a great solution, but hiring a bodyguard full time for the rest of a client's life wasn't in most people's plans or budgets.

All in all, it was something Marcus found frustrating. Since he'd been working here, he'd only dealt with one other stalking case, and with Paolo's help, they'd relocated the young woman and her mother...and so far, so good.

With all of that information swirling in his mind, he asked, "You want me to escort him to and from home?"

"For tonight, at least. Get a baseline. Leave him your cell number and we'll take it from there. I'm assuming he's going to need some kind of security system put into his place quickly."

"I can rig something up for tonight—get him to work in the morning and do something more permanent."

"That'll work, Marcus. Anything you need, let us know."

"Did you run a check on him at all?"

"No. Figured I'd leave that up to you." Styx clapped him on the shoulder, dismissing him, and Marcus headed back to his desk in the corner. He didn't spend a ton of time in the office—most of the investigators didn't—so this was just a place to store a few things and use a secured computer line. Granted, he did have that at home, but since he was close to his first meeting with Cole, he sat and started attempting to access Cole's information.

And he had half an hour to kill before he met Cole at the diner.

Many keystrokes later, Marcus came to one conclusion—Cole was clean. Too clean. That shit always made Marcus suspicious, when a random twenty-three-year-old gay guy showed up out of nowhere. No sign of parents. It was like he just bloomed in the middle of town.

Could be WITSEC, but Marcus doubted it. One call to his handlers and Cole would've disappeared. Which meant he could be running from someone and didn't want to tell Styx. Or he could be making all this shit up.

4

COLE SAT IN THE DINER AFTER WORK, THE WAY HE HAD COUNTLESS other times since moving to town. He wasn't hungry though, instead just drinking soda and waiting for a guy named Marcus to come meet him.

Styx had insisted on it. He'd stayed with Cole until he'd calmed down enough to work. And Cole had to admit that it was nice to feel like someone gave a shit about him. It'd been a long time since that had happened...and it was a whole different thing than guys like Mustang Man hitting on him.

It was a fact of his life—guys hit on him all the goddamned time. At one point, it'd been flattering and then it became part and parcel of a job he hated. Now, it was just empty. Sex wasn't something to enjoy—flirting was a commodity, and he played the game if it brought him customers with cars. But at night when he palmed his cock, the only thing that made him calm was picturing Styx together with the two men he lived with.

Cole liked Styx—the guy was hot. Even though Cole had tried to forget all about his libido, it sprang back to life when he'd watched a brief moment of affection pass between the three men. If he hadn't heard the rumors, which he guessed went long past rumors and firmly into the fact category, there was no way to look at those three men together and not know they were in love.

But the first time he'd seen the simple touch of Styx's hand to the back of Law's neck he'd noticed something in the tall man that had been pulled taut as a bow relaxed. Paolo was already loose, but the smile...

Holy hell.

Not ever going to happen for you.

Cole tried to picture all three men together, and even though he didn't have feelings like that for any of them, well fuck, that fantasy alone was a turn-on. Three big men, fighting for dominance. That got him going. Because it was real dominance, not the fake *you're mine for the hour because I paid for you* dominance.

He'd learned to put on a good enough show—he wondered if the day would ever come when the show wouldn't be necessary anymore. Because now, like then, he felt ruined for life. He wondered how many years it would take before that feeling went away. If it would at all.

Maybe he should feel guilty, thinking about Styx and his boyfriends the way he was, but it wasn't like Cole was trying to break Styx's triad apart. No, he wanted what they had, tried to picture himself involved with guys who cared about him. Granted, he'd prefer just one guy, but hell, thinking about the three of them together was hot.

Law had the same coloring as Styx, but his hair was a darker shade of blond and he was more classically handsome, while Paolo was dark-haired, younger, the perfect complement. And while Law was kind of a dick to him, Paolo was always cool.

And this Marcus guy? Well, if Cole had met him, he didn't remember.

"Here you go, babe." Tonight his waitress was Barbara—she always made sure he'd eaten enough and had taken to packing him extra food when he left. She put the new soda in front of him. "Ready to order yet?"

"I'm waiting for someone."

"Yell when you're ready." She smiled and walked away, and he looked up toward the front of the restaurant in time to see a dark-haired man cutting through the people milling around the front waiting to be seated. Cole wasn't sure what caught his eye because the man moved like a ghost, shifting through the congested aisles unnoticed. And how was that possible for a guy who looked the way he did?

Oh shit...this couldn't be *his* guy, right? Didn't Styx employ any regular-looking guys? Because the last thing Cole needed now were feelings of any kind toward anyone, but especially the man helping him.

For no pay.

Christ. He ran his hand through his too-long hair and thought about cutting and running. But the dark-haired ghost caught sight of him, stopped for a second. Cole saw a fleeting expression cross his face—suspicion, because Cole operated on that principle daily—and then the guy Styx had called Marcus set his expression to neutral.

Still, Marcus's lip had curled a little, as if he'd seen something he didn't like.

Great, we're off to a stellar start.

Cole nodded as Marcus got closer. Marcus's eyes narrowed slightly. He didn't like that Cole had spotted him before Marcus had spotted Cole. But he didn't know that Cole had radar for men who moved like predators.

No one else he'd ever spotted had made it look so good, though.

Marcus slid into the booth across from Cole, immediately shifting so his back was mainly facing the window. Cole assumed it was for the same reasons he always sat with his back to a wall—he never wanted to feel like anyone was sneaking up on him.

Finally, Marcus simply said, "You're Cole."

"Yeah. Marcus, right?"

"My boss sent me. Said he thought you might have some trouble."

Okay, so what the fuck kind of comment was that? Carefully chosen words indicated that Marcus didn't quite believe there was trouble at all—and he'd made it seem like Styx felt the same way. Like Cole was some crazy person who made up stalkers.

He reached into his pocket and pulled the note out, putting it on the table between them. "I didn't write that myself."

Marcus pressed his lips together as he read the note. "I'll need a handwriting sample."

Maybe they do this to everybody. Maybe they did it to every client who couldn't pay. But Cole felt like he was the criminal here.

Styx had believed him, seemed so concerned—or so Cole had thought. And he was typically very good at reading people.

Because now, Marcus? He had Marcus pegged. Someone, somewhere had hurt the guy badly enough to make him suspicious of every single guy from that point onward. That was usually a rich-guy thing, not limited to them, of course, but rich guys always thought guys like Cole wanted their money.

And he could peg Marcus this easily because he himself had the same goddamned issue. So he reached into the pocket of his work cargoes. Among the small washers and screws, he found a pen, pulled it out and used the place mat to write the exact words of the note, without referring to it (which he couldn't decide if that made him more or less innocent seeming)...but the message was burned into his brain.

He pushed the paper over to Marcus while meeting the man's dark-eyed gaze. "Next?"

Marcus made a pissed-off sound deep in his throat, then glanced between the two notes.

He's thinking that I could've had a friend write the note. Which, if he had friends close enough to do that kind of shit... "Do people often come to the agency with false stories?"

Marcus didn't look up from the paper. "Yes."

"Why? What's the benefit?"

"Attention." Now Marcus was staring at him hard. "Get people to feel sorry enough for you and you think they'll do anything."

"Like take on a case for free?"

"Exactly."

Cole's familiar anger rose, hot and fast. "Go fuck yourself."

He put down a couple of bucks for his soda and a tip, took the note and the place mat (because he didn't need the waitress in his regular lunch-and-dinner spot knowing this shit, the same way he didn't need a piece of paper telling him that he'd been a whore) and then he walked out.

The garage was a couple of blocks away—he'd left his Harley there and walked, since the day had been warm. He stuffed his fists in his pockets. For sure, he needed to hit the boxing gym tonight.

A truck pulled up alongside him, a big Chevy Tahoe. Black. Tinted windows. Really fucking subtle. Guy probably had a small dick.

Possibly small-dicked Marcus had already rolled the window down. "Cole, get in the truck—we weren't done."

Cole didn't stop walking. "We're completely fucking done."

But Marcus pulled the truck in front of him when he went to cross the next street, and it blocked his path. "Are you trying to kill me?"

"Are you trying to kill yourself?" Marcus asked calmly. "If you're really getting threats, you wouldn't make yourself such an easy target."

Cole hadn't stopped to consider that...or had he, and Marcus simply made him so angry. "I can defend myself."

"So why ask for help?"

Cole clenched his teeth. "I didn't," he ground out. "Styx offered."

"And you said yes," Marcus pointed out. "Now get in."

His voice was a command. Cole's body wanted to respond to it—which was a surprise.

Grudgingly, he got into the passenger's side, and Marcus drove off. "I'll take you home."

"My bike's at the shop. I need it for the morning."

"We'll pick it up and put it into the truck after we eat." Marcus drove them across town to a hamburger/hot-dog outdoor stand that didn't look like much, but turned out to have the best food. Cole had found a new place for lunch—except if Marcus came here regularly, it would be a place to avoid.

5

MARCUS PLACED THEIR ORDERS, THEN JOINED COLE AT A TABLE TO wait. There was a decidedly uncomfortable silence, with Cole staring somewhere over Marcus's shoulder. Marcus took that time to study Cole more because, when he'd first noticed him in the diner, the only thing he could focus on was that Cole screamed sex.

He wasn't overt about it—but he didn't have to be. It was in the way he moved, his body long and slim and muscled, his light-brown eyes, speckled with a little bit of green, glowed, and his hair was blond and messy.

Truthfully, he looked well fucked, and whether he was or not wasn't anyone's business. But actually it *was* Marcus's, because anyone in contact with Cole was a suspect, even Cole himself...and the sleepy-eyed twenty-three-year-old heart-breaker was a prime one in Marcus's judgment.

As if reading his mind, Cole narrowed his eyes slightly to stare at him, his posture tense. It got even more so when Marcus refused to break the gaze.

He heard, "Food's up!" and Cole glanced over, then slid off

the bench and went to pick up what must've been their order, obviously not comfortable with the scrutiny.

But Marcus continued with that scrutiny.

Cole was handsome in that *come fuck me* way. His face was a little flushed, his lips were full, and he looked like he'd just rolled out of bed after a night of fucking. In a T-shirt and jeans, he looked sinuous. Comfortable in his own skin. Like he'd be comfortable on Marcus's lap, his cock.

Fuck. Fuck *no*. Just what Marcus didn't need: a way-too-young-for-him mechanic with a shady past. Been there, done that.

He was never going to stop having a type, so maybe one day his type wouldn't be a fucking user. And as cool as the guy sitting across from him had seemed, he was getting something for nothing.

And that raised Marcus's hackles. But he ate—and watched Cole eat everything in sight. Marcus had ordered a hell of a lot of food and only half a milkshake remained. Cole brought the straw to his lips now and sucked in, and Jesus Christ, Marcus shouldn't have waited so long between getting laid.

Granted, he'd had no interest in getting laid before this.

His mood quickly plummeted. Most people he'd met—in the military and in this business—had a sad story. The ones who shared it readily were looking for sympathy. The ones who held back were a mixed bag, ashamed or lying or intensely private.

Or all those things, which made this job more than difficult. "Are you surprised Styx offered to help you?"

"Not really. But I don't believe anyone really does anything for nothing," Cole told him. Suspicious bastard, just like Marcus himself. Also, Cole's answer was a great way for someone who was running a scam to make himself appear innocent. "How long have you known Styx?"

Cole gave a one-shouldered shrug. "He brought in a busted-up Harley my second day on the job. About five months ago."

"Where were you before that?"

Cole's eyes flickered over him, like he was trying to decide if he could trust Marcus. "All over. I took some time and drove down the East Coast. Went to Florida, then made my way back up here."

"Were you working?"

"No. I'd saved up for the trip."

Marcus knew he was lying but he didn't push right then and there. "You had another mechanic job before this?"

"Yep."

"Do you even want help?"

"Styx seems to think I need it."

Marcus sighed. "And you're going to sabotage it?"

"I didn't think Styx would send a dick."

Marcus pressed his lips together. "Private dick, yes."

Cole rolled his eyes. "You've been waiting on that one for a long time, haven't you?"

Instead of acknowledging that Cole was right, Marcus handed Cole a card, saying, "So if you get more notes, you call me. That's my cell. Styx gave me your number. Anything suspicious, anytime, give me a ring. No walking alone like this anymore."

Cole stared at the card, thinking why the hell did he need this shit? He was basically on his own, which was pretty different from what Styx had implied. Then again, Cole wasn't paying. "Got it."

"I'll take you back to the garage now. What time do you have to be at work tomorrow morning?"

"Why?"

"I'm taking you," Marcus said.

How had they gone from the non-belief to the babysitting? "Ten," he lied.

"I'll be there at nine," Marcus told him with a smirk as he collected their garbage and tossed it as they walked back to his truck. He played decent music on the ten-minute drive, and neither of them spoke. "Where's your bike?"

"Around back."

"Let's put it in the back and I'll get you home. Then I have to check out your place."

"For what?"

"Security."

"Fine. I'll meet you in a second," Cole told him. Went around to his bike, got on it and drove past Marcus instead of loading it into the back. As he took off, he heard Marcus cursing, and he laughed.

The truck followed him all the way home.

6

IT'D BEEN A SHIT NIGHT. ONCE MARCUS GOT TO THE BASEMENT apartment Cole rented in a four-story house, it was obvious how angry he was. But he didn't say a word, just looked around the perimeter of the house, then followed Cole inside. He checked the window locks, then installed something without telling Marcus what it was. He did the same thing behind the door.

Finally, Cole had asked, "Are those going to go off if I open up the window or door?"

Marcus eyed him. "You need to keep everything closed until I get here. Use a fan if you get warm." And then he left without answering the question, making Cole feel trapped in his own apartment. Which, after his behavior, he probably deserved.

He used some of the free weights he kept in the corner of his room, then put his iPod on, set it to deafening and did some jump rope and shadowboxing until he was a goddamned sweaty, tired mess. Then he showered off and fell into bed... unable to sleep but too tired to let his brain work overtime.

He did, however, think about Marcus, flashing back to him

as his dick got hard. They'd sized each other up, and there was no denying the attraction simmering beneath—or because of—the adversarial nature of their first meeting and beyond.

They were also backing away as fast as they could. Well, Cole definitely was trying. But Marcus was a hard guy to shrug off. He was big, dark-haired, arrogant and hot. Everything that hit Cole's buttons, but when he'd had buttons to push. These days, things were different. He was practically a goddamned eunuch.

Except his dick hadn't gotten the message tonight. His mind circled Marcus, the man's gruffness. His thickly muscled forearms. Capable hands. They could hold him up against a wall while they were fucking. Dark hair dusted the muscles, his hands were big, nails squared.

Cole would get lost in those hands.

His voice was a rough, raspy command that made Cole stand up and take more notice.

Which pissed him off.

He wasn't going to be controlled ever again.

Sleeping wasn't happening, and he wanted to jack off, but he felt like that would be giving in to something he shouldn't.

The only thing that made him feel marginally better was that no one had pushed him to reveal more about his past. Not yet.

He wasn't scared of sex, but his experiences with it had nothing to do with enjoyment— not his enjoyment, anyway. He'd figured it wasn't in the cards for him to enjoy sex. At least, until this point, he hadn't met anyone he'd been willing to go to bed with. But thinking about Styx and his men together had definitely stirred something inside of him...and it was good to see that maybe he had a chance in hell of actually enjoying sex one day.

Before Marcus, before this, it was all function. Something he'd had to take care of, and those brief moments of bliss were short-lived. But at least he was responsible for his own pleasure. And pissed that his brain—and his dick—had chosen to make Marcus a part of it.

The last thing he thought about before falling into a restless sleep was that he still didn't know if he was going to set off alarms if he tried to leave his own apartment.

Of course, once morning hit, he tested the theory out by opening the front door at eight, once he was all ready for work.

Nothing.

So much for alarms. He strolled out to his bike and got on, only to find himself face-to- face with the now all too familiar black Tahoe.

Marcus stuck his head out the window. "Morning, sunshine."

Cole fought the urge to give him the finger. "I didn't think you'd be here this early."

"I'm paid to think." And then he backed the truck up, waiting for Cole to go first. Okay, he supposed that was a decent concession, not trying to force Cole to ride in the truck, so he sped off down the highway in the early-morning quiet. Once he pulled into the garage and parked and checked in, he saw Marcus's truck take off.

And then he got a text message. *Don't leave for lunch until I get there.*

Great. Now they were going to be lunch buddies.

Not if I can help it. And Cole did help it, ordering delivery from the deli instead of going out, and texting Marcus that he didn't need any lunchtime guarding. Then Cole spent the extra time working on the Mustang.

Cole had just started his work on the engine, after his boss told him that the guy paid extra to get the job done more quickly. Cole wasn't going to argue with the boss, so he'd turned up the music in the back of the garage, where the customers typically never came, and he lost himself in the work. During the late afternoon, he went to grab a soda from the vending machine, passed by his workbench and saw it. Another goddamned note. Same paper, and, this time, he recognized it for what it was immediately.

He pocketed it, refused to look at it because what the fuck would it change? When his babysitter/warden showed, he could have the pleasure...or maybe Cole would ditch it and tell Marcus that nothing happened, that just the brief body-guarding act must've worked wonders and scared his stalker away.

That way, no one would ever look at the note in his pocket.

God, he had nervous energy to burn—had to get to the boxing gym tonight or he'd just start to vibrate from nerves. He turned back to the Mustang because that, at least, would keep him level for a while.

He heard someone clear their throat behind him—he'd been bent over the hood, giving whoever it was a great view of his ass.

He looked over his shoulder and saw it was Mustang Man. He was unabashedly looking Cole up and down, a small smile on his face, and how long had the guy been ogling his ass? Cole hurried to lower the music. "Hey. I'll have it ready before the weekend," he started, but the guy just held up his hand.

"I know. Just wanted to see how it was going...and to see if you had recommendations for a custom paint job."

The same recommendations his boss could make. "Sure, yeah."

"I mean, I have a list," he continued. "But I wanted to see if you knew any of them personally."

Personally. Ah, back to that. He moved closer and took the list. The guy moved right next to him, pretending to be interested in looking at it over Cole's shoulder.

Cole thought about taking Mustang Man up on his offer. He was tall, not as tall as Marcus, or as roughly handsome, but fuck, Cole could pretend. Except...he got the uneasy feeling that the guy would put money on the dresser when they were done. And that's the only thing that stopped Cole from saying yes when, after Cole pointed to the custom garage he'd use if the car were his, Mustang Man invited him for dinner. At his place.

"Tonight?" Cole asked.

"Yeah. It's almost five."

"I work till six."

"Ah, come on, Cole, you can get off early, right?"

Real smooth, Mustang Man. "Really can't."

He handed the man's list back to him—Mustang Man palmed Cole's hand instead, smiling suggestively. "A home-cooked meal and a movie in the comfort and privacy of my place? Especially after the brutal day you've spent working on my car...it's the least I can do."

The guy was getting a little too close. Cole took a small step back as disappointment crossed Mustang Man's face.

"Hey, what? You're dating someone?"

He should've just said yes, but... "I don't date my customers."

"I'll be the best exception you ever make," Mustang Man promised him. He pulled a card out of his pocket, reached forward and slid it into Cole's front one, taking a nice detour to his nuts while doing it.

And *fuck*...because he looked over Mustang Man's shoulder and saw Marcus watching them. And Cole had been in this position enough times to know what it looked like, even when it wasn't what it looked like. Part of him wanted to prove Marcus right. Another part wanted Marcus to see right through him, and this, to get that what was happening here happened to Cole all the time...and that it didn't mean Cole fell into bed with just anyone.

Not anymore. And definitely not for money.

Marcus had let it slide when Cole told him he was ordering lunch in at the garage—and he'd confirmed that himself when he parked unobtrusively down the street so he could keep an eye on Cole's bike and the path to the diner.

And now, there was a customer's hand in Cole's front pocket. And Cole was looking at him with a lazy-lidded look—could've been just an act to cover embarrassment, but it looked more like something Cole was pretty damned practiced in.

Jesus. Should've known.

The anger and betrayal that ran through him was a complete overreaction to a total stranger, but, hell, Styx had wanted to make sure he wasn't getting cold. And right now, he was anything but.

He watched Cole extricate himself. The customer looked over his shoulder at Marcus and back at Cole, and he didn't catch what the guy said but Cole gave a tight shake of the head. After another few seconds of conversation, the customer was walking away, semiglaring at Marcus—who glared right back and headed to Cole.

Cole, who stuck his hand up and said, "I got another note."

"So you get your customers to comfort you?" Marcus demanded.

"God, you suck," Cole muttered, pulled the paper from his pocket and handed it over.

Since you can't stop being a whore, I'm going to make sure I redeem you.

"Does this phrasing mean anything to you?" Marcus asked.

"I don't know what it says—I didn't read it," Cole admitted, and for the briefest of seconds, Marcus wanted to believe everything. Then got immediately pissed at himself for thinking that.

"You know who I think is sending these notes? I think they're from a jealous lover."

Cole didn't exactly deny it, but finally he said, "I haven't been with anyone since I moved to town."

And after what Marcus had just seen, Cole's admission didn't hold much weight. Opportunities like the one with the customer probably happened all the time—Cole was young and single, and there was no reason he should say no.

"Why didn't you call me when you got this?" Marcus asked, trying to keep his temper in check.

"Because you don't believe me," Cole said calmly.

"Maybe it's the guy you were just propositioning," Marcus suggested.

Cole stared down at the wrench in his hand, then threw it against the wall. It landed on the cement floor with a loud clank.

"What—you were going to hit me with that?" Marcus scoffed.

Cole glanced at him. "For your information, that guy's been propositioning *me*. And no, I don't think he's the one leaving the notes. And yes, I was in danger of hitting you with the wrench."

Marcus smirked. "Got a lot of jealous sugar daddies in this town?"

"You're such a fucking asshole."

"Not an answer."

"Fuck. You." Cole walked away from him and Marcus hung around, watching him clean up his station, pack his tools up and strap them to his bike. Marcus followed behind him closely, making sure to check for anyone following them.

But there was nothing suspicious at all happening during that short ride.

Cole drove the bike smoothly up the driveway. Marcus parked behind him and caught up with him as Cole picked up his mail and a small package, juggling them along with his keys.

Marcus put a hand on Cole's forearm, and Cole stiffened at the contact. But Marcus didn't pull away, asking instead, "Any idea who sent that package?"

For a second, Cole looked like he wanted to shoot him a sarcastic comment, but something shifted quickly. He looked down at the package and back at Marcus. "There's no return address. I'm not expecting anything. You saw me pull in and find it."

Yes, Marcus had. He'd also heard the jangle inside the cardboard when Cole had picked it up, and now Marcus brought his ear to it and heard a low tick. Most likely, it was a pipe bomb set to explode when Cole opened the box, which would cause the most damage. But he couldn't rule out that it might go off when Cole simply put it down unopened.

He kept a steady hand on Cole's arm and took the box from him with a practiced pressure with the other. He held it in both hands and looked at Cole as he began to back away gingerly. "Take my phone from my pocket. Get into my truck. Call Styx's office and tell them I'm in the woods—that I need dry ice and you need your apartment swept."

"Why?"

Marcus stared into Cole's eyes. "There's a bomb in the box, Cole." Cole paled. "Put it down. Call the police and get away from it."

"I'll be okay."

"How?"

"I want to defuse it. I can learn a lot about a person from the kind of bomb he makes."

"You know how to defuse bombs?"

"It's what I was trained to do, yes." Marcus was good at defusing explosives, and typically, defusing people. "Please, Cole, take the phone, lock yourself in the truck and do what I asked."

Cole reached into his pants pocket and pulled his phone out. "Got it."

"Keys are in the truck. And there's a gun in the glove compartment. But if you don't know how to use it..."

"I know how to use a gun safely."

"Good. I'm going into the woods. Any danger comes, you shoot at it or run it over."

7

COLE'S THROAT WAS DRY WHEN HE GOT IN THE CAR AND FOUND the gun. He kept the safety on, balanced it on the middle console and called the office. At that point, Marcus nodded to him from Cole's front stoop and began to walk slowly but purposefully toward the woods.

Fuck. He prayed that someone would answer the phone quickly. Someone did, on the third ring.

"Phoenix, Inc."

"It's Cole—Marcus wanted me to call."

"It's Paolo. What's wrong?"

He told Paolo about the bomb, and the fact that Marcus was in the woods with the goddamned bomb. Paolo remained calm, told Cole, "It's all right, Cole. You're doing great. Just stay put. We're on our way. Want me to stay on the line?"

Cole wanted to say no but he couldn't say much at all. The panic crawled up his body, and he held the phone in a death grip.

"Cole, we're in our car, heading to you. Take a few breaths. It's going to be all right." Paolo kept his voice conversational.

"We're just stopping for the dry ice. Two minutes— we're down the street."

Cole knew exactly where they were. He looked around, saw nothing out of the ordinary. And the woods were quiet. On the other end of the line, he heard talking in the background—Law and Styx—and the hum of traffic. It was so quiet...he had to believe Marcus was still safe.

"Marcus knows what he's doing. He'll be fine," Paolo assured him, leading Cole to realize he'd been saying shit out loud. "And you're fine, yes?"

"Yes," he managed.

"Good. We're pulling in behind Marcus's truck. Is that where you are?"

"Yes."

"Driver's side?"

"Yes."

"I'm coming to the passenger's side, okay? Can you unlock the door for me?"

He glanced at the passenger's side window, and Paolo was there with the phone to his ear. He hung up as Cole clicked the locks, saw the gun on the console and took it in hand.

Paolo was obviously used to handling weapons with the easy way he checked the safety, and then placed it back in the glove compartment.

Cole turned to watch Styx and Law striding toward the woods with a small ice chest.

They stopped, whistled and then went in.

"Don't want to startle the guy with the bomb," Paolo said. "They know what they're doing. Law's coming back to check your apartment. If it's clean, I'm going to have a look around myself, then I'd like you to come in and tell me if anything's out of place."

"I can't stay here tonight."

"Definitely not."

"Can you defuse bombs?"

"I'm learning. I was a cop. I dealt with a lot of stalker cases. That's why I wanted to check out the apartment and your bike. Sometimes, they like to leave markers."

"Like a bomb."

"Markers are ways they can feel like they own you. Might be small—a sticker or something."

Fuck. He put his head back and breathed out as he watched Law amble out of the woods.

He gave a small nod in the direction of the truck, and Paolo said, "The bomb's defused."

They watched together as Law scanned the door of the apartment with a piece of equipment that Paolo explained was a heat sensor.

"Do you think there's a bomb inside the apartment?" Cole asked.

"No. I don't think the guy would leave a package if he could get in. And Marcus said his alarm sensors weren't triggered," Paolo explained. "But it's better to be safe."

Yes, it was. And when Law opened the door and went inside and nothing happened, Cole breathed again. Because having people take their lives in their hands because of him wasn't something he'd ever thought he'd have to deal with.

Paolo's phone beeped. "Law's coming out. He wanted me to go in and check it out before I bring you in. He'll wait by the truck. But everything's okay, Cole."

Cole knew it really wasn't, but he nodded. Paolo went inside, Law remained outside the truck, keeping watch until Paolo came out and motioned for Cole to come inside the apartment with him.

No wonder both men had looked so disturbed after being inside his apartment. Because, although nothing inside had been taken or destroyed, something *had* been left behind. Several pictures, of him and Marcus, arguing in the street, Cole getting into Marcus's truck...

He stared at them. His first thought was that he and Marcus looked like a couple. The way they looked at each other...yes, they were angry, but in each picture, the look in their eyes was...

Like we could've ripped each other's clothes off and fucked right then and there.

Ridiculous.

His second thought was *the person who wants to hurt me has been really close*...now he'd been where Cole slept. "Shit."

He wondered if Paolo noticed what he had about the pictures, and at first glance, yes, he had. Now, Paolo looked at the pictures again and said, "This isn't good."

His heart was in his throat. "What?"

Paolo sighed. "The guy's closer than we knew. If he just started stalking Cole, I'd never expect him to go from a note to a bomb. He's escalated...and before he sent the note. And it's one thing if he knew you'd hired PIs, but he thinks you and Marcus are more than that. And these photos confirm that."

"We were yelling at each other."

Paolo snorted.

"We just met," Cole continued.

Paolo shook his head slowly. "It doesn't matter—what does is that the stalker thinks this is real."

"Now what? Do I check in to a motel?" More money he didn't have but...

"No, that's not safe enough. We've got a plan—we've got to

throw this guy off track while we hide you. Because seeing all of us here..."

"I'll grab my stuff."

"Anything valuable you should take for sure."

He packed quickly under Paolo's watchful eye. It was a fact of his life that all his belongings were easily packable, small enough to fit on his Harley, and the rest could get shipped to him or go into storage. Cole didn't have a hell of a lot—his life could fit pretty easily into a couple of bags, so he took all of it. His bike and his tools—his wheels and the things that made him money these days.

In the small clearing in the woods, Marcus stood by the defused bomb with Styx at his side. He'd had the bomb finished by the time Styx and Law met him, but both men checked it as well, to be sure. And then Law went back toward the apartment to check it thoroughly, while Marcus remained with Styx, trying to come up with theories...and a plan.

"This guy's more than a stalker," Marcus muttered, more to himself than Styx.

"Unless he's been escalating the entire time and Cole never noticed."

"How's that possible?"

Styx paced a few feet and walked back. "The day Cole found the note...something had to trigger that. Cole lives a pretty quiet life—work, then home, rinse and repeat. He's been here just over five months. Where was he before that?"

"A road trip."

"And before that?"

Marcus glanced at Styx. "We didn't get that far."

"Something happened."

Styx was referring to the photos—Law had snapped pictures of the ones found in Cole's place and sent them to both men's phones. "I didn't believe his story."

He figured Styx really wanted to call bullshit on that, but to his credit, he didn't. Marcus felt badly enough, and he still wasn't sure what caused the response. Or he hadn't been able to, until he saw the pictures.

Had it been so goddamned long for him that he couldn't recognize pure, old-fashioned attraction anymore? "I'll figure it out, Styx."

"If it's a problem, I can take over."

"Reprimanding me?"

"No, but you need to get your head out of your ass, no matter what Cole's bringing up for you."

Marcus crouched down and studied the bomb again. "This wasn't made by an amateur."

"Then it's a good thing we're not amateurs either."

No, they weren't—he wasn't, and, maybe, for the first time since he left the CIA, he had the surge of adrenaline, a reminder that he'd been good at his job before he'd burned out. "I'll take him to the beach house."

"Better than a motel."

"I'll stay with him. Find out more."

"At this point, I think we'll investigate for you while you keep him buried. Obviously, this guy wants Cole for himself. If that can't happen, then..."

Cole's dead.

Marcus picked the box up and handed it to Styx. "Can you get this to Clint? There's something here I can't quite put my finger on."

"Yeah, sure." Styx clapped him on the shoulder. "Go get the story, Marcus. And remember, we all have a past."

8

It took hours to get to his beach house, mainly because Marcus went in circles, trying to lose an imaginary tail. He was good, but he wasn't taking chances. Not until he got fully settled into the case and there was a need to take them.

And you should've gotten settled into the case ASAP.

Beside him, Cole was really damned quiet. Marcus hadn't bothered trying to draw him out, mainly because he needed to think some things through himself. The last thing he'd expected was to have to go into hiding with his charge.

The last thing he'd also expected was to hear from Styx with news that made things go rapidly from bad to worse. "Did you hear from Clint?"

"Not yet," Styx told him. "Listen, we stopped by your place, like we said we would."

Marcus split his time between his apartment in town and the beach house, and he kept enough clothes and such at each that he could travel between them very light. But he'd asked the men to check things out, to grab his mail and make sure that things were all good on that front.

Now, according to what Styx told him, nothing was good. "We found the same kind of package, same bomb, at your place. Outside the door."

"Shit," he muttered, and Cole's neck snapped in his direction. "It's okay, Cole," he said, but hell, Cole didn't believe him. Marcus didn't believe himself at this point, so he decided to be honest. "Styx found the same kind of bomb at my place."

It was Cole's turn to mutter "shit" now.

"Listen," Styx ordered. "You make that kid feel protected, Marcus, and if you can't do that—"

"I can," Marcus told him tightly.

"Good. But from this point on, you're not just watching out for Cole. You're a client now, until we figure this out. We're all on this case, me and Paolo and Law, okay? And we'll pull Clint in too."

"I can handle it."

"But Cole can't," Styx reminded him. "We need someone to stay with him for more than simple protection—someone's got to take care of him emotionally. Can you do that?"

Marcus gave a quick glance in Cole's direction. Cole was staring out the window, his body language closed off. Both of them were being hunted now, and while it certainly wasn't ideal, it made Marcus that much more determined to figure out who the hell was doing this...and why. "You know I can."

"I do. I just needed to hear you say it out loud," Styx told him before hanging up. Just then, the turnoff for the beach house loomed on the right, a private, unlit road, perfect for these circumstances. The house was listed under an LLC, so no one would be able to trace it back to Marcus.

Finally, he pulled the car into the slightly raised garage and closed the door behind them. The reassuring beep of the alarm made Cole seem to relax slightly. "Come on—I'm sure you're exhausted."

"I won't be able to sleep," Cole murmured, but he got out of the car, grabbed his bags and followed Marcus into the house. Marcus tried to help but Cole waved him off, so Marcus held the door open and pointed up the stairs.

"Turn right—last door on the left. Safest spot for you, okay?"

Cole nodded, walked up, and Marcus waited until he heard the guest-room door open upstairs. He didn't need to check each individual room of the house. Instead, he only had to look at the bank of cameras that showed every room on its own screen.

He'd turn it off for Cole's privacy, focusing it instead on the windows. But this place was wired, one of Marcus's experiments, and overall, he was pleased with his hideout.

He was opening a soda when Cole came into the kitchen. So he slid the can to Cole, who took it and drank before he said, "I'm sorry you're involved in this."

"Always part of the risk."

"Really?"

"Really." It was, but hell, it was pretty rare a stalker was this advanced when he was called in. Paolo was right—this guy had accelerated quickly. "But we do need to talk about this more."

"About what?"

"The faster we figure out where this guy came from, why he might be following you, the easier it will be to catch him."

Cole sighed, looked like he was having some kind of internal battle with himself. Finally, he put the can down and said, "I think it has to do with my previous job."

He looked resigned as he said it, and Marcus nodded and waited with a patience he definitely didn't have. A few long moments later, Cole continued, "I used to get paid for sex." Cole swallowed hard, his cheeks flushed, but there was a fierce pride in his voice, like he wasn't going to let anyone make him feel bad about his choices.

Marcus admired that, even as he wondered if, somehow, Styx or the others knew this— or at least sensed it. "How old were you?"

"Is that important?"

"It might be. I've got to put together a profile of this guy. Age matters."

"Mine or the john's?"

"Yes."

Cole sounded resigned when he said, "I was just sixteen when I started randomly hustling when there wasn't enough money for the basics. Blowjobs in back alleys. Then, when I was twenty, after a lot of close calls, a guy I knew hooked me up with an agency. Said it was safer. I worked there until I was twenty-three. I left on my birthday. All those years, gone like a blur."

"Do you still have the information of the guy you worked for?"

"Yeah."

"Were your clients regulars? Age brackets—just a general idea. Does anyone stand out?" Cole closed his eyes and laughed with zero humor behind it. "No, that was the problem."

When he opened his eyes, Marcus was staring at him, not a trace of pity, but there was an expression he wore that Cole couldn't quite place. "I mean, most of them were married—

passing as straight. Or maybe they were bi, but in whatever world they lived in, being with a guy wasn't accepted. And their ages? Ranged from thirties to sixties." Cole swallowed hard, closed his eyes again and tried to differentiate between them, to picture a face, but they all flashed through his mind quickly, blending together in a sea of cloudiness and faked sex. "No one stands out."

"I'm guessing you only knew them by their first names."

If that. Some liked to be called Daddy, but he wasn't sharing that with Marcus. "Right."

Marcus motioned for him to sit. Maybe he looked pale— and he definitely felt shaky, so he slid out one of the modern steel chairs and put his palms flat on the table.

"Did you ever see any of them privately—like they'd see you outside of an agency appointment?" Marcus asked.

"No."

"Did you see any of them more than others?"

"I had a few once-a-weekers. Some once a month. For a little while, I had someone twice a month."

"Normal? Rough sex?" Marcus prodded. "Anyone who pushed you past your limits, even when you told them to stop?"

Cole couldn't decide if it was more humiliating or less to tell Marcus, "I don't remember. Are you happy?" Definitely more.

"Not especially. Did any of them hurt you?"

"They all hurt me," he blurted out, stood so fast and hard the chair he'd been sitting in fell back. He left the room. This was a mistake. He should've just moved, changed his name again. Eventually, he'd throw whoever this was hunting him off the track.

And there was nothing to say he couldn't leave now. Which was the best idea he'd had in a while.

Now it was time to share that with Styx, Law and Paolo.

Now was the time to cut them—and Marcus—free, and not let them get hurt because of his past.

He hadn't unpacked anything, had simply put his stuff on the floor and gotten his bearings. Now, he went to pick up the phone but there was no dial tone.

"For your own good," Marcus said from behind him. "I'm saving you from yourself."

"Maybe I don't need your saving."

"I think you're lying to yourself if you believe that."

Cole fisted his hands, shoved them into his jeans pockets, wishing he hadn't admitted what he had to Marcus. He hadn't told Marcus everything though, because there was something to be said for secrets. "I get it, Marcus. You don't approve of what I've done."

"I'm doing a job. What my personal feelings are shouldn't matter."

"It does when you're a judgmental asshole," Cole shot back fiercely.

"Hey, you're judging me just as hard—why's that?" Marcus challenged. "I was military and CIA, just like Styx and Law. But you're not giving them the dick vibe. So who do I remind you of...?"

He stopped. Cole blinked, stared at the floor for a long moment, like he was processing something important. When he looked back up, he said, "Yes...you remind me of someone."

"Tell me more."

"Fuck." He turned around, slammed his bag onto the floor. "Must've blocked it out."

That didn't mean the guy he was thinking of was the stalker—it didn't always work that perfectly. But it made sense as to why he'd been so hard on Marcus from the start—beyond the fact that Marcus had been hard on him from moment one.

At least he had a reason. He'd love to know Marcus's.

"You need to unblock, and fast," Marcus told him.

"I met a lot of assholes, just like you," Cole said. "Fuck you hard. I'm not ashamed of what I did. I survived. Maybe it wasn't in a jungle defending my country, but at least I wasn't taking from anybody. I wasn't stealing. I didn't give anyone anything they didn't want. I didn't hurt anyone," Cole finished, his face flushed with anger.

"Except yourself," Marcus pointed out.

"Let's not pretend it matters to you." Cole slammed out, but there was only so far he could go because of the threat. He was angry, not stupid. "Fuck, this isn't working."

None of it was—not the job, Marcus, leaving his past behind. He'd never tried to hide it as much as learn from it. The money had been good but he looked at sex—and himself—a lot differently. There wasn't enjoyment in it for him, not like there'd been for a lot of the guys who worked for the same service. And even though he still had urges, the thought of actually following through on them hadn't interested him a bit.

Not until Marcus walked in.

And yeah, that was working out well.

He stared out the back deck of the expensive beach house and felt like he had not that long ago when he'd been rented for the weekend, right along with the beach chairs and the surfboards.

Right after that, he'd quit the business. He'd worked a couple of odd jobs, mainly bartending. And finally, he'd agreed to work full-time as a mechanic, which meant he cut down on the bar hours to two nights a week. The pay wasn't as good as it had been when he was hustling, but it covered the basics.

He heard Marcus come into the room.

"Cole, look..."

"Didn't get enough out of your humiliation efforts?"

"I need you to tell me about the men you were with."

He wheeled around. "You're fucking kidding me."

"I think it would help if we could narrow down who might be threatening you."

Cole drew in a breath. "God, I don't want to do this."

"If you'd rather talk to Styx or Law about this..."

Cole met his eyes. "Yes."

Marcus could only nod. He wouldn't tell Cole that he'd get shit from Styx or Law— they'd told him to handle Cole with kid gloves and he'd failed on every single aspect. And it wasn't Cole's fault at all. "Okay."

When he turned to leave, Cole said, "Wait, no. I'm not bothering them. They're doing enough for me when they don't have to."

"So you'll deal with me to punish yourself?"

"Basically."

It was going to be a long goddamned night. Marcus put on coffee, set the monitors to alert him if anyone came past the road or the beach perimeters. He gave a quick look to Cole, who was lying on the bed, staring at the ceiling, before he moved the cameras to face the windows.

Still, he kept the sound on. For Cole's own good. He'd taken Cole's cell phone, and he'd know if Cole tried to climb out the windows. And then he thought about calling Styx or Paolo, especially Paolo, because of his experience with stalkers from his time on the force.

He called Law instead. In a quiet voice, he told Law what Cole had told him about his time on the streets, and Law seemed completely unsurprised. "Did you know?"

"Yeah," Law said finally. "Not for sure...but I just knew."

How? Marcus wanted to ask, but then he figured that maybe there was a lot about Law's past that he didn't know about. Maybe it took like to recognize like, and he tried to reconcile Law to Cole's past. "I'm having a tough time."

"Why?"

"Cole and I didn't get off to a good start. I didn't believe him. And now this.... I was suspicious. I still am goddamned suspicious, Law. So I don't know what to do," he admitted.

"There's nothing to do. Treat him the way you'd treat me or Styx," Law said tightly.

And that was probably the closest to an admission that Marcus would get...the reason why Styx felt so strongly about helping Cole. "Suppose he's pulling something?"

"Do you really believe that?"

"You don't?"

"Not for a second, Marcus. Neither does Styx. And before you tell me that we might be too close to this, trust me...we are. But that's a benefit in this case, not a hindrance. We'd know if he was pulling something. He's got nothing to gain from this. And he doesn't have the personality to plant a bomb. He doesn't know where you live."

That was true. Marcus was letting his own past color this case, and that was definitely a problem.

After a long moment of silence, Law spoke. "He had no idea of your background. I know you've got a hang-up about that."

Marcus didn't bother to argue—it was the truth. "He seems really sad."

"It's not an easy past to carry around."

"How'd you get through it?"

Marcus thought he'd pushed it with that question, was

surprised when Law simply said, "When you're with the right person, it all melts away."

Marcus hung up and ran his hands through his hair. If Cole really wanted to leave, there wasn't a lot he could do to stop it from happening...but Marcus had to impress upon Cole the life-threatening aspect of stalking.

Again.

And maybe get the stick out of his ass.

Maybe.

9

PAOLO

Paolo heard Law's cell phone ring in the kitchen. He was in the living room, trying to give Law a wide berth, since Law had been in a fucking terrible mood since they'd come home from Marcus's place. He'd been muttering and pacing, and Styx had simply watched him as well.

Now, Styx came into the living room and said, "That's Marcus calling him."

"Things okay?"

"I think Cole told Marcus about his past," Styx said.

Neither Styx nor Law had mentioned what Cole's past was, but Paolo had a feeling he knew. Both men had horrible childhoods, and they seemed to pull in the same kind of lost boys they'd once been. It didn't happen often, but when it did, it threw off Law's equilibrium something fierce.

By the time Law was hanging up with Marcus, Paolo and Styx had gone into the kitchen to be with him.

Law looked up at them, the laptop in front of him. "What's up?"

"Figured maybe it's time for bed," Styx said.

Law shook his head. "Too much shit to do."

Paolo's heart sank—it was so rare for Law to turn them down...and whenever he did, it meant he was definitely in a bad place. "Come on, Law—Marcus and Cole are safe for now. You need to take time before you burn out."

Law shot him a look, his jaw clenched tight.

"Yeah, he definitely needs it," Styx murmured in a tone that always got Paolo hard—and usually Law as well, but, this time, Law just shot them an irritable look and repeated, "I've got shit to do."

"Not tonight you don't," Styx told him.

Law slammed out of his seat. "I don't need a fucking corrective every time you guys think I'm upset over something. I'm allowed to be fucking upset or pissed off or whatever it is, okay?"

Paolo took a step back at the anger radiating from Law. "You are. Of course you are."

"Then leave me alone and leave me to it," Law told them both through clenched teeth.

He picked up his laptop and left the room, and Styx put his arm around Paolo. "Cole could be his brother."

"Jason?" Paolo had never seen pictured of him—Law's brother had been killed by their father when both were just teens.

"Looks just like him, based on the few pictures I've seen."

Well, that obviously explained a hell of a lot—not exactly a great thing, but Law hadn't protested them helping Cole—it was just bringing up memories that were already never far from the surface.

No matter how deep Law tried to bury them...it would never be deep enough, Paolo knew. And that hurt him as much as it did Law.

"That's not going to last long," Styx told him now.

"What? The anger?"

Styx nodded. "I give it an hour, tops."

"And then what?"

"Then we go in."

LAW

When he heard Styx and Paolo move upstairs, Law went back into the kitchen. Next to the bedroom, which was his favorite room in the house for the most obvious of reasons, the kitchen was his close second. Because he had multiple exits, a good view of the front and backyards...and it doubled very nicely if they couldn't make it to the bedroom.

He felt safest here, most especially when the safety he was used to feeling suddenly deserted him. And he'd been feeling more and more vulnerable the more he learned about Cole and his case.

He hadn't been surprised when Marcus told him about Cole's background. He hadn't liked letting Marcus infer his own background hadn't been much different than Cole's, but sometimes that was the only way to make people understand that it didn't matter where people came from. It only mattered where they were now...and in Law's eyes, Cole had made the break from his past, whatever the reasons.

Then again, Law knew as well as anyone that it was impossible to cut ties completely.

He hated stalkers. One of his best friends, Damon, had

been stalked for years by the man who'd raped him. Stalkers were goddamned bullies.

He found himself fisting his hands on his thighs. He'd hated pushing Styx and Paolo away, but it was all just too raw. And he hadn't been ready. Which was, of course, the point. He'd never be ready...

"Hey."

Law looked up to see Paolo in the doorway. He should've known, because Paolo never gave up. He was probably more stubborn than Law and Styx put together, and that was saying something. "Hey."

Paolo brushed past his chair, making sure a lingering hand passed across the back of his neck before pulling a beer bottle from the fridge. He used the edge of the countertop to open the bottle top and then leaned against the counter.

"I know you and Styx are pissed."

Paolo raised a brow. "I didn't say anything."

"You were thinking it."

"Guilty conscience?"

Law sighed. "Just when I think I've put it all behind me for good, I realize no, I've just put it away. Because you guys know I don't have to worry about it coming up. But then something like Cole's case comes up and..." He shook his head. "It shouldn't get to me. It's not even similar."

"It's about having no control. And Law, you didn't. Cole didn't. Both of you were forced into bad situations." Paolo sounded so reasonable. Reassuring. "It's okay that it's still there for you. I hate that I can't take it from you, but remembering it...I get why it'll always be there. But you're not in that place anymore. And you have to use me or Styx—or both—to make it better."

"Have to?"

"Unless you just want to wallow. But Styx isn't going to let that happen for much longer."

No, Styx would take Law over his lap at some point soon—because he knew Law needed it. Not for any other reason. And Law wanted it, but that would make the feelings come up harder and faster—he had to feel them before they went away. And that's what he didn't want to have to deal with, at all.

"What did Marcus have to say?"

"Nice change of topic," Law said wryly. Paolo took a pull from his beer, his lips pursing around the long neck. Law's cock hardened. Immediately. "Cole told Marcus about his past. Marcus didn't know how the fuck to handle it."

"But you told him."

"I did, yeah."

Paolo nodded and took another drink, then must've noticed the look in Law's eyes. His brow furrowed, and then he looked at the bottle. And Law. And Law's lap. "I take it you're not interested in the beer."

"Not especially."

"I see."

Law spread his thighs on the chair, the outline of his dick through his worn jeans making it more than obvious how turned-on he was.

Paolo took another drink as he walked over toward Law. Finally, he handed the beer over. Law took a long pull, but he never took his eyes off Paolo, especially when the man dropped to his knees. He swallowed the beer, put the bottle down as Paolo undid Law's jeans.

"Paolo, I—"

Paolo put a finger to Law's lips. "You don't have to. Not with me. Not ever, okay? Now lift, babe."

Law accommodated him, let Paolo push the jeans down,

managing to free Law's cock and balls but still completely trapping his legs in the denim. Law was about to mention that when Paolo deep-throated his cock, without warning, and Law grabbed the seat of the chair and groaned.

Closed his eyes. And then Styx, who'd come from fucking nowhere, was behind him, rubbing his shoulders. Not saying a word.

"Where's the *I told you so*?" Law bit out.

"Never needed one before, babe," Styx reminded him. "That's not the way this works."

Law knew that, he really fucking did. He let Styx pull his arms behind his back and hold them there while he kissed Law's neck, then murmured, "His mouth looks so good on your dick, doesn't it?"

Law nodded his agreement, barely able to breathe correctly. Paolo was holding his hips, not letting him move, and when Paolo finally did release him, it was only so Styx could position him, forcing him to stand, holding on to the counter.

Paolo moved in between Law and the cabinets, taking his cock in his mouth again, while Styx's lubed cock entered Law. He cursed.

"So tight, baby," Styx murmured as he pushed in farther.

God, yeah, Law felt that. Styx was big, and Law didn't bottom often. But every time he did, he wondered why he didn't more often, because it was incredible to be filled like this. And he was, with Styx brushing his prostate, making Law cry out. The sensation of Paolo's mouth and Styx's cock was too much for him, sending him over the edge in that way he'd needed so desperately. The way his lovers forced him to see he needed. When he came hard in Paolo's mouth, he felt Paolo come against his legs and Styx, minutes later, throb inside of him. He half collapsed against the countertop and he let the two men he loved more than life itself take care of him for the rest of the night, forcing his mind away from the past and focusing it firmly on the present.

10

MARCUS SLEPT ON AND OFF, BUT BY THE TIME THE SUN ROSE, HE was awake and making breakfast. Cole came down to the kitchen more growly than he'd been the night before.

Marcus figured that now wasn't the right time to talk to him more about the men from his past. Instead, he watched Cole shovel in some eggs and coffee and then begin pacing. All that nervous energy and there was nowhere for him to burn it off.

Marcus didn't have any cars or bikes for him to fix here, but he did have a gym. He'd converted two of the bedrooms, knocking down a wall, adding in punching bags and various other items used in boxing, since that was Marcus's favorite workout. He'd stopped short of getting a ring, but he had mats on the floor to mimic an actual ring's size.

It was obvious that Cole worked out. He wasn't bulky, but he was strong and muscled.

"I've got a gym set up in one of the bedrooms," Marcus offered, and saw Cole's eyes light up. "It's got more boxing stuff than anything but—"

"That's perfect," Cole said. He went upstairs to the guest

bedroom and came out in shorts and a T-shirt with the arms cut out. He strolled past Marcus to the gym but didn't close the door. Seconds later, loud music shook the house, the kind of earth-shattering heavy-metal, old-school rock that shot through Marcus's body like a jolt of electricity.

Curiosity got the best of him, and he followed the pounding beat of the music like it was some kind of pied piper. Cole was hitting the small punching bag with an intensity—and a focus —it was pretty damn incredible. He must've gotten in a hundred hits per minute, lost in the motion, the repetition and probably the music as well. It made Marcus's hands itch to join him, but if he were honest with himself it was more than that, more than wanting to box.

He'd been drawn to Cole from the start, and pushing him away wasn't working. Would bringing him closer? Or would that just cause a whole other set of problems neither of them needed?

But Marcus was tired of questioning, of wanting what he couldn't have. At this point, there was no real reason he couldn't reach out to Cole.

Cole stopped punching the bag and turned. He didn't look surprised to see Marcus, and Marcus wondered if he'd heard him over the beat of the music. He held up his gloves and jerked his head toward the makeshift ring, a question in his eyes. Marcus nodded and held up a finger. He went downstairs and changed into clothing similar to Cole's and returned, taping his knuckles quickly and sliding on the boxing gloves.

Cole had gotten so deep in the zone that he hadn't noticed Marcus's approach. Nothing to do with the louder-than-hell music—that was how he always boxed, iPod or not.

The anger that coiled deep inside of him had moved to strike so many times over the past few days that it had exhausted itself. Now, there was only "feeling"...and it made him nervous, so he had to wear that down too.

He'd laid himself bare to Marcus, and Marcus, to be fair, had been called out for some of his past too. But Marcus hadn't sold his ass for money, then had to admit it to the first guy he'd been attracted to in forever.

Inside his head, Cole cursed to the beat of his fist on the bag.

Fuck.

Punch.

Fuck.

Punch.

Fuck.

The rhythm got stronger, until he realized that Marcus was behind the large bag, holding it in place so Cole could get better hits in. "You realize I'm pretending this is your face, right?"

Marcus looked unimpressed. But he did move away from the bag and a little too close to Cole. Without warning, Cole turned and punched him, his glove catching Marcus on the side of his jaw.

It was more satisfying than he'd imagined. He dodged, bounced on the balls of his feet, waiting for Marcus to retaliate. Needing him to.

Marcus bared his teeth and started to move. He was light on his feet for such a big man. And together, they'd moved onto the mat while circling each other, a silent agreement that they were going to finish this fight, one way or another.

Jab.

Duck.

Punch.

Marcus was good, although Cole got in several shots. Marcus seemed caught between admiration and anger.

"Tell me what you're pissed about," Marcus demanded.

Last night, Cole had dreamed of the past, woken in the middle of the night, restless and worried. He was also tired and angry, and he'd paced the floor, trying not to look out the windows into the darkness. Paranoia was something he'd never had to deal with when he was selling his body. Most of his clients wanted desperately for him not to recognize or remember them. He'd never had anyone obsessed with him or anything—he'd had regular, steady clients, but he'd spent the money almost as soon as it came in. "I'm losing everything. My job...my income. I've got nothing."

"Thought maybe you'd saved some money from your previous job." Marcus was jabbing him verbally, purposely, forcing Cole to get it all out.

But even though Cole continued punching, he didn't take the bait immediately. "Yeah, I spent it on reckless things like rent and food," he said dryly.

"Plus a random road trip. Even so, maybe you weren't very good then. Because you should've been making more."

Cole stopped, incredulous. "So what, you're my pimp now? You're judging my performance? I wish I knew you then—you could've negotiated my contracts."

"Better than you did."

"Dude, seriously, keep pushing it."

"I'm really worried."

Cole rushed him, but he wasn't that much of a match for Marcus. Marcus caught Cole as the man bear-hugged him, punching at his back. Marcus made a soft grunting sound and then hooked his leg around the back of Cole's so they both went down hard on the soft mat.

Cole was about to tell him that this was not allowed in boxing, but one look at Marcus's eyes, the feeling of his cock hard against Cole's own, and he didn't give a shit about fighting anymore.

Marcus rolled them, ending up on top of Cole. Kissing him. And before Cole knew what fucking way was up, he was kissing Marcus back.

Finally, he pulled away. "Son of a bitch—you goaded me into this."

Marcus didn't even look guilty. "You wouldn't kiss me any other way."

"For good reason." But Cole was rubbing against him. "Hope you have condoms."

"I do," Marcus told him. "But I know you get tested regularly. That you're clean."

Cole froze and then his adrenaline surged. He bucked Marcus off him, jumped to his feet. "Fuck you—my medical history records are private."

Marcus was on his feet again too. Cole swung, but Marcus was ready, caught Cole's fist in his palm and held it. Too long, because Cole caught the back of Marcus's knee with his foot and, together, they went tumbling down hard because Marcus wouldn't let go of him.

"Does it make you a big man, having me admit that I get tested a lot? That I always did? That I doubled up on condoms, refused a shitload of money to bareback? That I'm still going to be paranoid for the rest of my life, Marcus?" he hissed.

Marcus stared up at him. "You sold yourself for sex. Probably dropped out of high school, same old story about your parents not understanding you or hitting you or abandoning you. The usual bullshit. Rough trade. The lure of the customer, the easy money, was too much to resist."

"You got that last chunk wrong." Cole was sick to his stomach. He rolled off Marcus and went to walk away. He didn't expect Marcus to tackle him, but he ended up flat on his back, Marcus on him. "Is this your idea of professionalism?"

"I give what I get, Cole. My job is to figure out what the fuck is going on with you."

"What's going on is you leaving me the fuck alone. Someone tried to kill me—or do you think I planted the bomb myself?"

"Definitely not."

Marcus wasn't the only one who could read people. "Just because you got fucked over and didn't realize you were paying for it until it was too late doesn't mean you get to project all your shit on me."

Bingo. Marcus stilled. Blanched. Of course, Cole had gone too far—it's what he did when pushed. And now he was trying to ensure that Marcus stayed as far from him as possible.

He was done hanging around with people who made him feel used. "Call Styx. Tell him thanks but I'm going to do this on my own."

"I'm not officially working the case anymore."

"Then get off me...and let me go," Cole growled.

"I'm a client myself. Your case has tangled me up in it. You know that."

"You can stay here and watch yourself."

"Whatever former trick misses your cock put a bomb inside my apartment," Marcus informed him. "So you aren't going anywhere until we figure out who this could possibly be."

"I can't fucking stand this." *Or you.* "Just get off me. You've heard of personal space?"

Marcus snorted, but he pushed off the floor, leaving Cole flat on his back.

Shaking.

And he didn't want Marcus to notice, so he rolled himself onto his side, hoping it was less apparent, that Marcus would just leave the room.

But the panic must've been worse than he realized. Because Marcus was wiping down his face and neck with a cool cloth, talking to him in a calm, soothing voice. His body against Cole's wasn't panic-inducing at this point.

"I'm fine," he croaked.

"I know, Cole." Marcus was serious. He pulled Cole up to a sitting position, had him lean against Marcus's shoulder, helping him drink some juice and refocusing on the world in general.

Cole turned suddenly to face him. They were inches apart. "I didn't like saying things to hurt you."

"I started it," Marcus said quietly. He slid his hand behind Cole's neck, murmured, "And here I go again. Can't help myself with you."

Cole closed his eyes when Marcus's mouth took his. There was nothing soft about the kiss and Cole was glad. He didn't want soft coddling because that would've been fake bullshit from Marcus. And they'd already laid their cards on the table.

He groaned into Marcus's mouth, a complete and utterly real sound that he couldn't control. Marcus's hand tightened until Cole was on his back again, Marcus's weight on him.

Cole's leg came up around the back of Marcus's thighs, pressed himself up against the big man. It was the beginning of the end...and suddenly Cole couldn't think of any reason to stop it from happening.

. . .

Marcus stared down at the handsome man under him. He'd been surprised at Cole's strength.

Hell, he was surprised about Cole in general. He was sweating, and Cole was covered in a thin sheet of sweat as well. Both of them were breathing hard.

Jesus, this was foreplay if he'd ever seen it.

"Why are you stopping?" Cole asked. Because Marcus had pulled back abruptly to make sure Cole was okay. Because he could barely breathe himself after making out like a fucking teenager until he almost came in his pants.

"Because I want to make sure you're okay," he said honestly.

That seemed to disarm Cole, whose eyes flashed with an expression akin to vulnerability.

Or the closest he'd allow Marcus to see of that emotion. "I am."

"No, you're not. But that's okay, Cole. It is." Marcus sucked the tender spot along the younger man's collarbone, making him gasp. He had a feeling it'd been a long time since anyone had done anything in bed for Cole to simply bring him pleasure. And as badly as Marcus wanted to be inside of him right now...Cole wasn't ready. Marcus still had some making up to do.

He'd start now. He began kissing his way down Cole's body as Cole semi-froze, his eyes following Marcus's every move. Watching Marcus lick and nip his way down Cole's chest, circling his belly button with his tongue, then dipping lower. Spreading Cole's legs. Sucking hard along his inner thighs until finally he took Cole's balls and mouthed them gently but still with enough pressure to put Cole through the roof.

"Holy fuck, Marcus." Cole grasped at the floor, obviously looking for anything to grab hold of to keep himself in check. But that wasn't what Marcus wanted him to do, and he spent the next God knew how long driving Cole completely wild. He took Cole's cock into his mouth, swallowed it down, deep-throating him to the root. Cole's wild cries were music to his ears. He hummed around Cole's cock, wanting to give him plea-sure and take nothing in return. Cole wasn't there yet, and this was the furthest Marcus would push him.

He pulled back and laved the head of Cole's cock while stroking him with an undeniable rhythm.

"Dammit, Marcus...please."

"Keep begging," Marcus encouraged.

"Bastard," Cole panted.

Marcus laughed and suckled Cole's balls into his mouth while holding Cole's hips down.

"Please, Marcus...I need to come...fuck. Please..."

Marcus came in his goddamned pants because of Cole's begging, so he figured it was only fair to let Cole. He sucked Cole in deeply, then stroked him fast until Cole stiffened and then shot down his throat, all the while calling Marcus's name.

11

After he'd made Cole come hard enough to turn himself inside out, Marcus carried him into his bed and held him as the rain pattered on the deck outside the half-opened window.

Neither man cared that they were sweaty and sticky. It didn't matter. The original tension had bled away. That didn't mean it wouldn't be replaced...and Marcus really didn't know what the hell he was hoping to accomplish with this. All he had known was that he'd wanted Cole, and it had been a hell of a long time since he'd wanted anyone this badly.

Cole was watching him now. Maybe waiting for an apology, or maybe not. Either way, Marcus owed him something of an explanation. "I need you to understand why I was so hard on you. Why I'm going to keep pushing you on all of this."

"Okay," Cole said, his voice slightly hoarse.

Marcus tightened an arm around him, a reassurance. "Look, I came into Phoenix with several specialties, one of which is being able to tell who's bullshitting the agency and who's being honest."

"So Styx and his partners thought I was lying?"

"No, I think Styx thought I needed a kick in the ass. Because instead of being able to pick out honest men the way I once could, everyone was guilty." He looked at Cole, whose expression softened a bit. "And I wouldn't have done it had I known the seriousness of this one. But I guess the point is that I couldn't see clearly, and I'm sorry you were the one who almost had to pay for that."

Cole nodded. But he didn't say anything about accepting Marcus's apology. Instead, he said, "Paolo said this guy's been watching me for a while."

"Right. And when he saw us together..."

"But he wrote the note before I met you, Marcus. Before I talked to Styx."

"And you've been friendly with them since you came to town. So whoever it is never saw them as a threat," Marcus mused. Which meant he'd traced them back to Phoenix, or discovered they were a committed threesome. "What happened in the hours before you saw Styx?"

"Regular day at work. Fixed cars, dealt with customers."

"Any of them yell at you?"

Cole's eyes flashed after a second. "Definitely no yelling."

"Then what?"

He stared at Marcus. "That guy—the one you thought I was propositioning? He was there in the morning, before the note came. Actually, just before."

"And the customer was pulling the same stuff he was the day I saw you together?"

"Yes."

"Was he aggressive?"

"Not like he was when you saw him. But nothing I couldn't handle."

"And then I stepped in on top of that and escalated it. You

betrayed him by talking with someone else...and then he saw us fighting and..."

"You couldn't have known."

But if I'd believed you... "You're not dating anyone?"

Cole flushed. "No."

"How long's it been?"

"I don't date."

Join the club. "Last guy who picked you up?"

"What makes you think they picked me up?"

A little touchy there. He'd probe that, but really, he didn't understand how Cole couldn't see why he'd be wanted. "You don't look like you'd have a shortage of men after you."

It's a compliment, Cole. Marcus was asking questions but he was also flirting, which made him feel decidedly like flirting back.

"You don't look like you'd have a problem either," he told Marcus, who let a slow smile cross his face.

"True. But most people assume I'll make the first move."

"Don't you?"

"No."

"Why's that?"

"I see who's circling me. And then I look for the ones who aren't. And that's who I go for."

"You like the chase."

Marcus chuckled, a husky sound that stirred Cole's dick. "I do, but I like the catch better."

He was so close—closer than Cole might've ever let him get otherwise. He reached up and put his hand on the back of Marcus's neck, pulled him closer, saying, "I like the catch too."

Whether Marcus kissed him first or not this time, it didn't

matter. Marcus took control soon enough, but not in a way that made Cole feel anything but aroused.

His hand moved to thread in Marcus's hair, losing himself in the kiss. Marcus's hands were on Cole's hips, holding him close, their cocks rubbing together. Between that friction and Marcus's tongue, Cole came again with little effort, spilling all over Marcus's belly. This time though, he'd pulled Marcus to climax with him, and that made him inanely proud of himself as he watched Marcus revel in the loss of control.

12

COLE FELL ASLEEP FOR WHAT MUST'VE BEEN THE BETTER PART OF the afternoon, because when he woke, it was dark out and the house smelled delicious, like a home-cooked meal, and it made his stomach growl. He jumped in the shower quickly, then pulled on shorts and a T-shirt before heading down to the kitchen.

He found Marcus at the stove, with several pots going, plus the table set already, appetizers lining the middle of the table. "Are you expecting company?" Cole asked.

Marcus looked over his shoulder. "Yeah, you."

Cole's throat tightened. "You're cooking for me?"

Marcus turned around to face him fully. "I can't take you out on a date yet. I figured this is the next best thing."

"You're treating this dinner like a date?"

"That okay with you?"

Cole simply shrugged at his question, and turned and headed back into the living room, but not fast enough to hide the small smile that bled through. He couldn't explain it, but

Marcus made him feel alive, more so than he ever remembered feeling.

"Go ahead and sit. This is all ready."

Marcus plated the steak and the vegetables and potatoes for both of them. Took out the crusted garlic bread. Poured them sodas since they had to be alert. The appetizers were shrimp and cheeses and meats, and between the two of them they pretty much cleaned all the plates.

Afterwards, Cole insisted on helping clean up, which made quick work of things. And then the two of them were half passed out in food comas on the couch. Cole's legs were draped across Marcus's lap...it was like a fucking dream except it was really happening.

And just think, a few short days ago, you were prepared to hate him. And he definitely hated you.

"Thanks for all of this," Cole told him. "I mean, the dinner. And then being patient with me. I'm not a prude but..."

Marcus waited patiently for Cole to finish. He wasn't sure if he should put it all out there, but he figured it was certainly time. He took a deep breath and said, "I've only had sex for money, Marcus. I was a virgin when I started. And after I'd gotten out, I'd had enough sex to last the rest of my life."

"But you didn't. Trust me." Marcus rubbed a hand over Cole's bare shoulder.

Relief surged through him. "I do."

"Good. Then it's time to change your experience. Ready?"

Cole was more than ready. Adrenaline pounded through his body as Marcus stood, pulling Cole up with him, then forcing him to walk backward until he hit the wall. He pressed against Cole, asking, "Is this what you want?"

"Yeah."

"Use me, baby."

Cole tilted his head and stared. Marcus continued, "Come on. Pick me up. Talk dirty to me. Fucking own me while I'm owning you."

Cole smiled. Oh yeah, he could do this. He grabbed Marcus's hair in his hands, fisting it hard. "You're mine tonight. Got it?"

"Yeah," Marcus breathed. "You gonna use me hard...put me away wet?"

"I want you to do that for me," Cole told him.

"So it's all about you?"

"Yes."

"Good." Marcus reached down to the hem of Cole's T-shirt, tugging it up and over his head while Cole released his hold momentarily. And then Marcus was kissing him, his strong hand splayed on Cole's bare back. Cole shuddered at the sudden contact, moved a hand back up to thread through through Marcus's thick, dark hair. The other rubbed Marcus's jean-clad hip, then moved up to touch the bare skin along his side.

"What do you like, Cole?"

God, it had been about pleasing everyone else for so long that he didn't even goddamned know what turned him on.

"Did you come with your clients?" Marcus prompted.

"Yes."

"Because you lost yourself and fantasized, or was it pure biology?"

He'd been sixteen years old when he'd started hustling to pay the rent and eighteen when he'd gone full-fledged to the streets, and at that age, a good stiff wind could've made him hard. "The last one."

And that made it worse—he didn't even like what was being done to him and still his goddamn body betrayed him.

Marcus traced the muscles in his arm, concentrating deeply. Cole felt the first stirrings, like he did whenever Marcus was this close and concentrating on him as if Cole was the only thing in the world that mattered.

Cole tried to do that with his clients and he guessed he faked it well for the first few minutes, because after that, once the fucking began...who the hell noticed?

Cole knew Marcus would notice.

There'd be no way to escape noticing Marcus during sex. That made Cole's gut twist with fear and worry...and excitement. He swallowed hard, and Marcus smiled and said, "So treat me the way they treated you."

"What?"

"Use me to explore. Discover. That's what they were doing, right? You were safe for them."

Cole hadn't thought about it like that. It put a spin on it that, while he wasn't entirely comfortable with it still... "Yeah, I'm the Mother Teresa of fucking."

Marcus snorted, but his eyes remained serious. "You shouldn't feel guilty about what you did. I just don't like that you felt forced."

"I don't want to go there now."

"Where do you want to go?"

Cole stared into his dark eyes that were ringed and flecked with black. "I don't know, Marcus."

"Then trust me."

After a long moment, Cole nodded, and Marcus added, "I'll take good care of you. And I'm also going to blow your goddamned mind."

Cole wasn't even really remembering to hang on—but it didn't matter. Marcus was controlling everything, and there was no way to stop his full weight from driving Marcus deep inside of him. The constant rub and thrust of Marcus's cock against his gland was making him fly.

And he wouldn't let Cole look away. Their eyes locked the way their bodies were—with Cole squeezing the shit out of Marcus's shoulders and Marcus holding Cole's hips hard. They'd both bear marks from this.

Cole wanted Marcus's marks all over his body. "Marcus, please... Yeah... Just..."

Marcus continued his rhythm, driving in deep and hard and smiling. Growling Cole's name. Finally he said, "Baby, you're going to come when I say so."

Cole nodded with a pleading gaze and finally a gruff plea of "yes" escaped from his throat. He was surprised to hear it— silence had been his thing, if the john would let him get away with it. Otherwise, he had to fake it.

None of the sounds he made while Marcus was fucking him were fake. He was half sobbing, cursing Marcus while begging him to *please fuck him harder*.

"Guess we know what you like," Marcus managed as he bared his teeth. They were both sweating, straining to hold themselves back.

"Marcus, goddammit."

"Come, baby. Come all over me."

Cole couldn't tear his eyes off Marcus, as he shot, hard enough to see stars alternating with Marcus's smile, a smile that urged him on. He kept coming, his ass contracting around Marcus's dick. He cried out. Cursed. And then got to watch Marcus fucking lose it. And it was the best thing ever.

His expression went taut, then relaxed as his body went rigid. His hips jerked erratically. His cock pulsed inside Cole, who basically went over the edge again. "Jesus Christ, Marcus."

Marcus held him tightly, groaning as Cole contracted around him again.

Cole wasn't sure how long he stood there. His head bowed against Marcus's shoulder, Marcus supporting him. But at some point, Marcus pulled out of him, then slid an arm around his waist, another under his ass and carried him to the couch. Cole was still wrapped around him when Marcus sat, with Cole straddling him. Marcus kissed him, an openmouthed, messy tongue kiss that got Cole hard. Marcus chuckled into his mouth.

"What?"

"Your response time—the beauty of youth."

"Think you can keep up, old man?"

Marcus's brows raised. "You just bought yourself a hell of a lot of trouble."

"Is that supposed to scare me?"

Marcus shook his head and broached him with his fingers. Cole groaned and pushed against Marcus's fingers, surrendering again to Marcus, fully. He rubbed himself against Marcus, and it wasn't an act, his mind didn't go to a scene a john asked for.

No more johns—only Marcus. For as long as he was in danger. Cole couldn't dare hope for beyond.

He also couldn't help but ask, "Does this happen a lot—with clients?"

"That they end up with my fingers in their ass? No."

"I didn't mean to offend you. It's just...this job forces you to get close to people...so I thought..."

"I don't get close to people," Marcus said tightly, and Cole's heart froze...until Marcus put a hand on his cheek. "But I guess one good save deserves another."

"Definitely."

"The way I grew up...I kept to myself. Not at first. I was too trusting and then I lost that."

"And I'm sure the military and the CIA really made you soft and cuddly again," Cole said, with just the right trace of sarcasm in his voice.

"You think I'm soft and cuddly?"

"Totally." Cole rolled his eyes. "Retraction—I think you are, under all that gruff shit."

"Yeah, well, I think the same of you."

"I'm not gruff."

"No. You're a complete wiseass."

"You don't seem to mind," Cole pointed out, since Marcus's arm was in place like a steel band, holding him there. Urging him closer.

"I happen to speak wiseass," Marcus informed him.

13

MARCUS WAS PACING. RUNNING HIS HANDS THROUGH HIS HAIR. Mumbling to himself. Every once in a while, he'd snap his fingers and then shake his head and start the whole process all over.

Cole stretched on the couch, still trying to process what happened last night, all while hiding behind a movie marathon of *The Fast and the Furious*.

Finally, Marcus did stop talking to himself and dialed his phone instead. "Yeah, what you think? Prince? Yeah, yeah."

There was some military-like speak in there, stuff he recognized from movies but really had no clue what it meant. All Cole knew was that Marcus moved in the same way all three of the guys who owned Phoenix, Inc. did, a way that belied their training. And it was a way Cole definitely appreciated.

"Thanks... No, makes it worse. But, hell, now we know what we're up against, right?" He glanced over at Cole, who made a show of keeping his eyes glued to the TV. "Thanks, man—appreciate it."

Cole continued to stare at the TV until Marcus's thighs guided his view instead. He looked up and said, "Hey."

Marcus crouched down. "Sorry to be all in my head today. I get that way when mulling shit over."

"Does that include last night?"

Marcus smiled. "Nothing about last night was about work. The phone call was."

"I want to know."

Marcus made a motion for Cole to move his legs. Cole did, and Marcus pulled them back down along his lap, his strong hands massaging Cole's feet. "I want Hooker Headers on my truck."

"You're just trying to keep me busy."

"I've plenty of other ways to do that."

Cole let Marcus take his time with the massage. Because he knew more questions were coming his way, ones that could put the broken pieces of the wall up between them again.

Finally, Marcus said, "The guy who's after you is probably an agent—most likely FBI. Maybe former military."

"How do you know?"

"I recognized a few things from the bomb. Everyone's got a slightly different way of making them, but you can—I can—tell a pro from someone who gets their skills from the Internet. This guy has a signature. Sometimes that can help us trace who he is. So the next question is..."

"You want to know if anyone I fucked seemed like they were military or a fed."

"Basically, yes."

Cole closed his eyes and went back to the place he never wanted to go back to. He could picture the room—a cheap motel off the interstate where he took most of his clients. The rooms were paid for by the service, but of course they weren't going to pay for something more expensive or for any place that might get their escorts arrested. "It was my birthday." He felt Marcus's hand squeeze his knee a little harder as if to reassure him.

Cole opened his eyes because he had to see Marcus's face when he told him this story. "My last birthday was the day that I quit the service and started traveling down to Florida. I'd had two clients already. Normal stuff, nothing sketchy and nothing out of the ordinary. I showered and waited for the new guy to show."

He looked down at his hands and realized he'd fisted them together. He opened his hands, trying to relax them by rubbing them against his thighs, but there was no way he was going to relax. He decided to just blurt out the rest. "I didn't remember any of this when you first asked me. I mean, I blocked a lot of it out—it's not like I have memory loss. But until the pieces started coming together, and you mentioned possible military, I'm thinking the third guy from that day... He was the final straw, and after him, I quit the business...and I think he could be the one who's following me now."

Marcus's eyes were dark with anger, but none of it was directed at Cole. His next words were ground out. "What makes you think it's him? Did he hurt you?"

"Not like that. Not like you're thinking." Cole shook his head. "That's why I didn't even think of him."

"Tell me, Cole. I promise I will make this better."

Cole took a deep breath. "He wore dog tags. I saw them outlined through his shirt. It was tight and he was pretty built. He had a tattoo that looks kind of military-like but I didn't recognize it. And he was really nice to me—he actually talked to me. Wanted to know if I was really okay with this, if anyone was forcing me to do this. He told me that he didn't normally use escorts but that it was just easier for him because he was away so much. Normally, I'd just shut them up, get it over with, you know? I'm looking to get paid, not have a therapy session. But I don't know—maybe because it was my birthday or the way he spoke to me, but I broke down. I told him I wasn't being forced, but I couldn't do it anymore. That it wasn't him. And he actually smiled. He fucking paid me. And I walked out and I left him sitting on the bed, and I got on my bike and I went back to my shitty apartment, packed all my stuff and headed out."

He knew what Marcus was going to ask next. But he couldn't bring himself to say that he didn't remember the john's name, that he'd never remembered any of their names because that would've made it all too real. And as if Marcus knew what he was thinking, he ran a hand up his calf and said, "Just tell me about the tattoo."

An hour later, Marcus was staring at a picture he'd drawn with Photoshop on his laptop. He'd hated putting Cole through it, but it hadn't taken long before Cole told him that the picture on the screen was the man he'd walked out on. They'd started with the tattoo because Marcus figured that would be the easiest. As soon as Cole described it Marcus knew they were talking about a Marine. But there wasn't anything special or distinctive about the tattoo—there was no platoon number or anything that could distinguish it from thousands of other Marine tattoos, so that wasn't going to help them.

That's when Cole sighed resignedly and began describing the Marine. Between Styx and Law and Clint and himself, they had a ton of ways to circulate this picture, but facial recognition was the most secretive. It could take days, even weeks, and that didn't guarantee a hit. But it was better than anything they'd had so far.

"Doesn't make sense, Marcus." Cole sounded frustrated. "The guy was really nice to me. Why would he suddenly start stalking me? If he was that pissed, wouldn't he have just beaten me up before I left?"

"Stalkers come in all different flavors. That's the scariest part—you never know what's going to set one of them off. Maybe you looked like his high school boyfriend. Maybe you weren't supposed to walk out. Maybe he left you his phone number on one of the bills he paid you with and you never noticed. Or maybe he's got some kind of God complex and he thinks he saved you."

"It's not like Mustang Man was the first customer to hit on me."

"Maybe it's the first one he saw." Marcus scratched his chin. "Maybe it took him a while to find you, Cole. We're assuming the guy followed you this whole time, but that might not be true."

Cole nodded pensively. "So, what, I was supposed to pine away for just him or something?"

"If you try to make sense of this, babe, you'll drive yourself crazy." Marcus cupped the back of his neck and pulled Cole close. At first, the younger man hesitated, but then he settled in, halfway onto Marcus's lap. "It doesn't matter why he's doing it. It has nothing to do with you. You did nothing wrong."

Cole nodded. "Ironic that he's the one that made me quit the business and head this way, right?"

He'd lived a lifetime with Marcus in the few days since Cole had received that first note. Time spent here in the beach house seemed to speed their relationship up and yet time somehow slowed down as well. Because everything was simply focused on the two of them...and them on each other. Whether it was the danger of the situation or the forced close quarters, Cole didn't know, and for the moment he didn't care. He'd broken through a wall he'd never thought he'd be able to scale, and it was dangerously close to crumbling completely. How the hell had he gone from hating Marcus to being in the guy's bed in such a short period of time?

Maybe this was all a fluke. But no...they'd had sex more than once, and it had gotten better each time. And now, Cole lay staring at the ceiling, Marcus's body flush to his. There had been no question about Cole going to sleep in the guest room since that first night, not when Marcus had put a heavy arm across his chest, keeping him in place. Marcus wanted him, and he made no bones about it. Tonight had been no different.

Before Cole could let himself get pulled into other worries, Marcus started shifting. At first glance, Cole thought he was waking up, but then it became apparent he was dreaming. A long moment later, Cole could easily see it wasn't a happy dream.

Marcus mumbled into his pillow. Then he turned over, and the mumbling turned into several clipped and cryptic statements. Then a long silence, followed by a soft, stunned declaration of "fucking no", and then Marcus opened his eyes and stared straight ahead. Whatever he was seeing in his mind's eye gave him that destroyed expression. Marcus was involved in a deeply personal struggle when he closed his eyes, and it made Cole practically growl with a possessiveness toward Marcus that he hadn't thought possible. He wanted to protect the man who'd started bringing him back to life...he wanted to keep Marcus's monsters away.

He started slowly, waited until Marcus seemed to wake a little and his breathing calmed. And then Cole rubbed the back of Marcus's neck and finally, Marcus turned into him, seeking comfort.

They were both still naked, and the immediate proximity had Cole's body flaring to life. At first he felt guilty since Marcus had obviously been in the middle of a nightmare...until he noticed that Marcus's cock had responded pretty quickly as well.

Maybe you can take his mind off things.

Cole believed that Marcus might not even realize that Cole had seen the nightmare. And with that, the protectiveness that had surged minutes earlier was back in full force. Cole reached back and grabbed for condoms and lube, even as his free hand slid to wrap around both his and Marcus's cocks.

Marcus moaned softly, his face still buried against Cole's shoulder.

"Yeah. Gonna make you feel better," Cole murmured against his ear. Marcus's hips jutted at those words, his pleasure more than obvious. And although Cole wanted to move slowly, he wanted more. Needed that...and he wasn't about to wait.

He pushed Marcus onto his back and straddled him. Marcus was watching him now, his cheeks flushed with sleep and arousal. Cole grabbed Marcus's wrists and put his hands close to the slats in the headboard. Understanding, Marcus gripped the lowest slat, remaining immobile and open to Cole.

Cole rolled a condom onto Marcus. For the briefest of seconds, Cole flashed back to his hooking days, but this was such a different experience. Because Cole was getting immediate pleasure from helping Marcus...the arousal had spiked through him to an almost unbearable level. He used his fingers and the lube, opened himself while Marcus watched hungrily, and then he lowered himself onto Marcus's cock.

"Jesus…Cole," Marcus groaned when Cole bottomed out on his cock. Cole only paused for a second before he started to move against Marcus, making sure to hit his gland repeatedly.

And although Marcus was letting Cole take the lead, it was clear that Marcus was in to it. He'd depended on Cole to pull him out of whatever he'd dreamed about. And Cole had no problem topping from the bottom. Not that Cole had been passive with Marcus, but now Cole was most definitely in charge, pushing all of Marcus's buttons…and in turn, all of his own. It was a heady feeling, and he was in this so damned deep with Marcus he wasn't sure he'd be able to escape unscathed when the time came.

But he refused to let himself go there, instead choosing to focus on the extreme jolts of pleasure making his cock leak. Marcus's knuckles whitened as he held on tightly to the headboard. Their eyes locked as Cole's orgasm coiled low in his belly. But Marcus came first, with a loud groan and a curse, his hips finally jutting up hard. And that motion, the look on his face, pushed Cole over the edge, coming in hot spurts on Marcus's belly until he collapsed onto Marcus's chest and closed his eyes.

14

STYX

FOR THE THIRD NIGHT IN A ROW STYX found LAW WIDE-AWAKE IN bed and Paolo nowhere to be found.

"What the fuck is going on here?" Styx demanded. "No one sleeps anymore and no one tells me shit. Why are you and Paolo so upset?"

Law stared at him. "I don't want to sleep because I don't want to dream. Paolo's worried about this case."

"So why isn't he saying anything to me?"

"He doesn't like to say anything until he figures out what's bothering him."

"I'm going to go get him."

"Hey, bring me up some ice cream."

Styx gave Law a smile over his shoulder. He'd do anything for the man—ice cream was easy. But Paolo was not going to be easy.

Styx found him staring out the window facing the woods. He didn't want to sneak up on the man, so he waited until Paolo turned his head a little and said, "It's okay, Styx. I know it's you."

"Am I losing my touch?"

"I heard Law say ice cream." Paolo smiled sheepishly as he turned to face him. "I also heard you yelling."

"Come on—let's grab some ice cream, go up and sit with Law, and you can tell us what you're thinking."

Paolo helped him carry up the ice cream, which Law accepted eagerly. Together, they discussed the information that Marcus had learned. The computer next to Law was running searches, but hell, it could take forever with the sketchy intel they had. And that wasn't Cole's fault. Paolo was grateful he was able to give them as much as he had.

"Okay, so let's say this guy's actually a Marine, like his tattoo presents him to be," Paolo started.

"A Marine who also likes to pay for sex," Law pointed out with his mouth full of ice cream. "That's not the most upstanding kind of military man. First of all, the uniform gets you laid, so the fact that this guy actually went out of his way to pay for sex means he's got some kind of issue."

"Issue, yes. But stalker?" Paolo shook his head. "I'm just not seeing it."

Even though Paolo didn't bother to point out that he had the most experience of all of them with stalkers, neither Styx nor Law forgot. "So we've got to come up with a new profile. If we've been targeting the wrong guy this whole time..."

"Then the right guy's had plenty of time to plan." Paolo looked troubled. "I think we should move Marcus in here."

"I think that's the worst idea ever," Law told him before spooning more ice cream into his mouth.

"Just because you hate people—" Paolo started.

"I don't hate you," he said to Paolo. And then he motioned

to Styx. "Or him. Most of the time." And then he shifted so Styx couldn't grab him.

"You are just itching for it, aren't you?" Styx asked.

"Isn't that obvious?" Law said.

"Yes," Styx and Paolo said in unison.

"Thanks to fucking God, because I was getting ready to dance around naked."

Styx sat back against the pillows. "Don't let us stop you." And then he glanced over at Paolo, who was actually smiling. "But before that happens, Paolo, you should call Marcus and talk with him about this. I'd like to get his take on it. Maybe Cole's too."

And then he sat up straight, snapped his fingers. "Wait a minute. There's something... the day I was there, right before the note showed up, Cole almost got into a fight with another mechanic. I figured it was just territorial pissing, you know? Fighting over a customer. Plus, Cole's kind of a hothead and I know how that goes." He looked pointedly at Law, as did Paolo.

"You can all stop looking at me," Law told them. "Or you're not getting that dance."

PAOLO

Paolo had gone downstairs to get Law more ice cream—he claimed that dancing made him hungry—when a movement on the back lawn made him still in the downstairs hallway. He moved quietly, opening the hall closet by pressing the code without taking his eyes off the back lawn and pulling his weapon out.

"Where's my ice cream?" Law asked from behind him in a

stage whisper. Good thing Paolo had heard him coming or he would've shot the fucking floor.

"There's someone on the property." Paolo took his weapon from its holster and began walking towards the back door. Law stopped him, a heavy hand on his shoulder. "Get the fuck off, Law."

"You got nothing to prove."

"I know that, dickhead."

Law snorted, then looked out the back window. "There's someone back there."

Paolo fought an eye-roll. Styx came into the kitchen at that point and called to them, "There's someone on the property."

"Oh for the love of God," Paolo muttered. He shook off Law's hand and slid out the back door quietly. He figured the two numbnuts would follow shortly, and rather than keep himself in the possible line of fire, he opted instead to run toward the woods. He heard the rustle as if the intruder was running away from him. Paolo picked up speed, but just as suddenly the noise stopped.

"The guy just fucking disappeared."

Styx said what they were all thinking. "Only guys I know who can do that are spooks."

Law sighed, looked at Styx. "You think someone's after you?"

"It's been too damn long. What the fuck would anyone want with me?" Styx asked.

"Yeah, because you're so innocent."

"It's too big of a coincidence," Paolo told them both. "The guy who was out there was looking for Cole. There's only two ways this can end, and I only like one of them."

15

———

THE NEXT MORNING, MARCUS AND COLE LEARNED ABOUT THE man on Styx's property. "They think it's our guy," Marcus confirmed.

"Dammit." Cole punched the table with his fist, enjoying the sting of pain. "What the fuck, Marcus? What's he going to do? He's gone from zero to sixty in like five minutes."

"I think we've got to believe Paolo's theory—this guy's been following you for a hell of a lot longer than you've realized. You said yourself that you weren't dating...weren't having sex. Maybe that kept him at bay. Maybe he figured you were being faithful to him," Marcus explained.

It made sense. But the thought that some random psychopath had been following him for months...fuck. Had he looked through Cole's windows? Watched him at the diner?

"This can't go on," he muttered.

"It won't. We're searching for that Marine," Marcus soothed. "Don't worry. We'll get him."

"By hiding?" In Cole's estimation, it seemed the only way to draw his stalker out was to keep doing what he'd been doing to get the stalker's attention in the first place. Before Marcus and the bomb. "You need to let me back out there. At least during the day—draw him out, get him comfortable. Maybe I can get him to approach me if you and Styx and Law and Paolo stay out of the picture. Make it seem like I'm on my own again and lonely."

Marcus glowered and shook his head. "Fucking. Forget. It."

"Look, Mr. Large and In Charge, that's only going to work in the bedroom."

Marcus's smile was a handsomely predatory one, and it made Cole's stomach flip. In the good way.

Even so, he put up a hand. "That wasn't an invitation."

"Sounds like one." Marcus advanced. Cole's dick homed in on that and told Cole what— who—it wanted.

Still, he backed up. Marcus kept moving forward, and Cole's back hit the living room wall.

Marcus put his hands on either side of the wall above Cole's head. Locking him in place without touching him at all. Yet.

And that's all Cole wanted him to do. They'd come so far in a short period of time, but that had happened easily because they were locked away in paradise together. What would happen once they were spit back unceremoniously into the real world? Hell, at this rate, it seemed like it would never happen.

The reality was, Cole was broke. Or he would be soon, because he wasn't working and he had no safe place to live. The longer he hid from the world, the worse it would get. Once they were back out in the real world...well, Marcus hadn't made any promises. To be fair,

Cole hadn't asked for any, but...

"You're thinking too hard," Marcus informed him. "It's my job to stop that."

. . .

"Really? I'm going to need to take a look at your Phoenix, Inc. instruction manual to see if that's really part of your job," Cole murmured later, his face buried in Marcus's chest. Marcus laughed, the sound that had been so unfamiliar just a couple of short weeks ago coming far more easily now.

He'd only had the nightmare twice. A record for him. Cole had seen them both, but he hadn't asked about them, only sought to soothe Marcus back to sleep. Marcus was grateful he hadn't pressed...but until he talked to Cole about it, Cole wouldn't understand why making statements about putting himself in danger would freak Marcus out so thoroughly.

He forced himself back to that day, that technically successful mission that still felt like a failure...a mission so full of contradiction that he couldn't get past it, spilling it all out for Cole to hear. Cole, who simply listened to the story in its entirety, without asking questions. Without judging.

With Cole's hand on his heart, Marcus told him everything.

Goatfuck missions happened nearly every day... Sometimes, even when the mission went well, it wasn't all good. Like his last one in the CIA. The joint task force he'd been a part of had gotten out the kidnapped ambassadors, but the people they'd had to leave behind in that small village...

"Aid is coming," the FOB had said repeatedly in his ear, and the men he was working with were just as torn as he was. Because aid was *not* coming before the rebel soldiers, who'd been going town by town, pillaging and killing.

He beat himself up over it—logically, he knew there was no way to get a hundred people on this small helo, no way to lead them to the jungle while fending off an army of soldiers with his five-man team. This wasn't goddamn *Tears of the Sun*. And when you looked at a hundred people out of the thousands being killed...

"It would've been something," he'd told the shrink fiercely.

"And you feel that saving the ambassadors was nothing?" she'd asked.

"Not what I said."

"What else could you have done?"

"They all died. We saw it happen from the helo. Those women... They knew. And they fucking comforted us before we left." His voice had broken a little. "We made the pilot hang and watch until it was all over. Our penance. The least we could do."

"And you beat yourself up about it every day since."

"Yes."

"What you think will make it go away?"

"Nothing. And I couldn't stay in a job to keep helping when I felt like all I was doing was pretending."

It was the last thing he'd said to her on his very last visit, because hell, going over and over it wasn't helping, and nothing she said could convince him to feel differently.

The only thing that could possibly help was doing more good than harm with his new job. At least now, working with Styx and Law and Paolo, he could save one person at a time. It was much easier to handle one person at a time.

And Cole was looking at him like he understood everything. Jesus, Cole might actually be able to, too...because Cole might've sold his body, but at times Marcus felt like he'd sold his soul...his humanity. And he wasn't sure he'd ever get it back.

But Cole had helped him get it back. He might be street smart and nowhere near innocent, but he'd still somehow retained enough joy...a joy he gave freely to Marcus. Cole touched a part of him that he thought he'd wound up and wrapped so tightly nothing would ever touch it again. And he'd hated that at first because it scared the shit out of him.

And he told Cole all of this, and Cole teared up.

"You're too good for me," Marcus managed.

"You're not getting rid of me, all right?" Cole wrapped his legs around him.

"That's not what I'm trying to do."

"You can be a dick, sure," Cole said wryly. "Both when you're being protective of yourself and the men in your life who you trust..."

"Like Styx and Law and Paolo."

"Yes," Cole agreed. "You guys are going to be a part of each other's lives forever. I like that kind of loyalty."

"You've got that same loyalty from me—you know that, right?" Marcus asked, and Cole nodded. "And no one's taking you from me. Understand? I'll do anything I have to in order to keep you safe."

"I don't want anything to stay on your conscience."

"Let me tell you something—this guy threatening you? My conscience will be clean, whatever I need to do to stop him."

"You're going to kill him?"

"Cole, it's you or him."

Cole looked sick. "I know."

"The nightmares I have aren't because I saved someone. They're because I didn't save *enough* someones." Marcus paused. "I know you saw a couple."

"You have them every night, Marcus," Cole told him quietly. "Shit. Sorry. I didn't realize—"

"It's okay." Cole's hand closed around his forearm. "I don't want to embarrass you or make you talk about something you don't want to talk about. God knows you've been patient with me. But I don't want to lie to you...or make you think you're not having them."

"I'll sleep somewhere else if they bother you."

"I don't want you to sleep somewhere else. They only bother me because you look like you're in pain."

"How can I be in pain? I don't even remember them," Marcus said, trying to blow the whole conversation off, and to his credit, Cole let him. Until later that evening, when Marcus woke up screaming and Cole wrapped his arms around him and murmured that everything was going to be okay.

"There was a time when it wasn't," Marcus told him. "It wasn't that long ago, and I wasn't sure things were ever going to be all right again."

"And now?"

Marcus found Cole's hand in the dark, looked into his eyes. "I think maybe it could be. But I'm not there yet."

Cole simply tightened his arms around Marcus until the he let himself fall back to sleep against Cole's chest.

16

For the next few days, things were nearly perfect. Perfect, if Marcus could forget that they were hiding out because a crazed stalker was trying to kill them both. Which he did manage to do some of the time. He cooked for Cole, and they worked out, sparring and boxing, learning each other's moves. At night, or sometimes all day, they learned each other's bodies. It was an incredibly intimate arrangement, maybe a first for both of them, and since they couldn't exactly back away, they just barreled forward into each other.

They didn't talk about families or jobs, beyond Cole's work at the garage and Marcus's work at Phoenix. It was as if they'd both been reborn when they started those jobs, or as if they both wanted to be.

And it was good. Really good. Between the movies and the books Cole borrowed from his shelf, and the music Cole blasted, Marcus couldn't remember a time when he'd smiled more. There were no new leads, but then again there were no new sightings of the psycho either. And so it was far too easy to pretend that they were safe.

Marcus thought he knew better than to fall into that trap. But spending time with Cole was easy. Despite the age difference—and Marcus began to realize that Cole had lived a lot more than his age would have it seem—they had a lot in common. Sharing what happened on that fateful mission had brought that out.

At night when dusk fell, Cole and Marcus would walk along the beach, Marcus always with his weapon. They passed families and dogs, and Cole would get his pants wet every single time because he liked to walk in the cold water barefoot.

And then, slowly, Cole began opening up about his family. The first time was when they were having dinner, and Cole made a comment that beef stew had been his father's favorite dish. He hadn't seemed upset about it, and he ate the stew easily so Marcus had to assume it was a good thing. A couple of days later, they were watching a movie, *Gone in Sixty Seconds*, and Cole pointed out the Shelby Mustang and said, "That was the first car my dad and I worked on together."

"Your dad was a mechanic?"

"Yeah. He had his own garage for a while, until he got sick. And my mom, she died a couple years before that so we were alone. I don't think either of them had much family—at least I'd never met them. Still haven't."

Cole's story was similar to the ones that he'd heard in boot camp and beyond, because most of the military men he knew, especially the ones in Special Forces, seemed to have the shadiest backgrounds imaginable, as if that somehow catapulted them to become some kind of heroic being. It made a lot of sense, actually. Abused kids had to have a lot of situational awareness—they had to learn to read people early and quickly to avoid danger. They had to learn self-defense techniques. They had to learn to be invisible. They'd grown up with warfare, so the warfare of the military was not new to them. It was simply a different kind of war.

A couple of days later, Cole told him, "My dad was an alcoholic. I would just tell everybody he was sick, and I guess being an alcoholic is like being sick. The times he wasn't hitting me or passed out drunk, we'd fix cars together. Until he lost his business and there were no more cars to fix."

"Is that why you don't drink?" Marcus had assumed there was some kind of issue since Cole steadfastly refused any kind of alcohol, although he didn't seem to have a problem when Marcus had a beer.

"It never does anything for me. I've tried it, but I figure I have the gene of addiction, so why tempt fate?" Cole shrugged. "Relax, I'm not one of those reformers."

"I'd stop drinking around you if you want me to. It's not a big deal to me."

"Thanks," Cole said softly, and Marcus took that as a yes and so he put away the beer, because he only had them occasionally, and they drank iced tea or soda or coffee.

One night, Cole told him, "Sometimes it's the smell of the alcohol, you know? It's like one whiff of bourbon could take me right back to being six or seven or ten or twelve, and knowing when his hand was going to come down across my face."

And that's how it was when Cole opened up—a slow-blooming plant, each leaf bared to him a gift. Marcus didn't take them lightly.

Cole thought about all of those days, and he wasn't sure how he survived. It had been a really long haul for him. But losing everything at sixteen and then spending the next year barely treading water had taught him many things. And it wasn't like the years before that had been so great.

Now he turned to Marcus and said, "I pretty much watched my dad drink himself to death. He lost everything. I tried to help with the garage, but it had started to go downhill when I was too young to really get a handle on all of it. At least my dad taught me everything he knew about cars before things started to go wrong. I remember being like three and going underneath the chassis with him. He used to quiz me and I didn't care because I just loved spending time with him."

"What happened to make him start drinking?" Marcus asked.

"Part of it was returning from the military—at least that's what I heard. I was only six when he came back and he seemed fine to me. I guess military men know how to put on a good act." He looked at Marcus, who shrugged and nodded. "And then when my mom died, things got really bad. I know my dad felt horrible about the drinking, about not taking care of me the right way. Toward the end, he stopped hitting me and yelling at me. He just got really quiet and he slept a lot. I should've known."

"No, you shouldn't have. You were a kid. I'm so sorry, Cole." Marcus's hand was steady on his shoulder.

"Yeah well, I'm sure growing up for you was pretty different."

"Money doesn't solve problems. Sometimes it creates more."

"True. Money couldn't have helped my dad. He would've just thrown it all away with the booze and the gambling. And hell, I wouldn't have been able to manage it. Today, maybe."

"Is that what you want to do? Open your own garage?"

"It's way too early to think about that. First, I've got to try to get my job back."

"I know Styx talked to your boss. He said he'd try to keep it open as long as he could, and that he'd keep what was happening to you under wraps. I guess he told the rest of the guys that you had a family emergency."

"It's not like I'm allowed out of the house for anyone to know differently." Cole shrugged.

"It's not forever."

For some reason, that hit Cole a lot harder than it should. Of course he didn't want to be in hiding from the stalker forever, but it only served to remind him that his time with Marcus, at least like this, was limited. "I know that. And I'm grateful for what you guys are doing."

Marcus looked at him funny, but the expression passed quickly and Cole told himself that it was nothing.

17

LATE THE NEXT AFTERNOON, MARCUS RAN DOWNSTAIRS TO THE now-beeping perimeter monitor in time to see a flower delivery truck leaving the driveway. He clicked a picture, getting the license plate and the company's name, and he quickly called them.

"Hey, did you guys just drop off something at my house?" He gave them the address and they confirmed that, yes, indeed they did.

"The card says that it's from your brother," the owner of the flower shop told Marcus. "Was the card not included? I'm so sorry."

"Not a big deal," Marcus said smoothly. "He has messy handwriting anyway."

The owner laughed. "Oh they all do. But he called it in, so I was the one to write the note."

"Thanks again." Marcus hung up and tentatively opened the door. Just because the flowers were legitimate didn't mean that the deliveryman had been. It was a simple floral arrangement, wrapped in clear plastic, tied with a ribbon, a slightly more masculine vase filled with dark-red flowers and lots of greens.

Cole was at the door next to him. "Who the hell sent a dozen long-stemmed red roses?"

Almost as soon as he said it, his expression went taut. Marcus told him, "Cole, you need to move back, okay?"

Cole did as Marcus asked, and Marcus caught the quick look of fear in his eyes before he retreated. Marcus didn't waste time, bending down to listen. He looked in the clear vase, but he saw no signs of a bomb or any other kind of tampering. Gingerly he pulled the card out—the one the stalker obviously put in to replace the original—and saw the message, written in neat bubble-like script.

I'm so close to saving you. Don't worry—no one can hide you from me for long.

"The good news is it's not a bomb. The bad news is this guy's tracked us here. This house isn't safe."

Cole took it better than he expected, asking, "Where do we go now?"

"I can only think of one good option," Marcus told him. And he hoped the men he was about to invade felt the same way.

Cole wasn't exactly thrilled with the answer to his question, although he did agree that moving into a house with three weapons experts and Marcus would serve to protect him well. So sometime after two that morning, after driving for an extra hour in case there were any tails, Marcus led him through the attached garage and into Paolo, Styx and Law's kitchen.

Cole felt like an idiot, of course. These men were already protecting him for free and now he was completely freeloading off all of them.

All three men were up and waiting for them. Styx took his bag and Paolo asked how he was doing.

"Sorry to intrude like this" was all he could think of to say.

"You're not." Paolo spoke so firmly that Cole chose to believe him. Except the look on Law's face told a different story. Law was still standoffish, just like he'd been to Cole every time he'd visited the garage, disapproving—even although that last part might be Cole's conscience talking.

"I'm just going to head to bed, okay?" Cole told Paolo, who in turn led him to a bedroom where Marcus and Styx already were.

"We'll be secure in here," Marcus said. "There's only one small window and it's got bulletproof glass."

Cole didn't want to ask why the windows in this house were bulletproof, but he supposed all of these men were too suspicious for their own good. For that, he was grateful. "Sounds good to me. I'm a little tired."

Styx nodded at him. "Treat this like you would your home. I know this is a rough time for you, Cole, but please know we wouldn't have asked you guys to stay if we didn't want you here."

Cole waited until Styx left and closed the door behind him before telling Marcus, "Law can't stand me."

"That's not true. Law is just extra suspicious, especially around anybody trying to get close to his guys."

"I'm not trying to get 'close to his guys'," Cole said, hearing the defensiveness in his own tone. "Like I said, I'm just tired."

"Come on and get into bed." Marcus pulled down the comforter, and Cole crawled in gratefully.

He wasn't even sure if Marcus had gotten into the bed before he closed his eyes—stress sleep, most likely—but he was wide awake two hours later. He didn't want to wake Marcus, and he noticed there were lights on in the hall, so he carefully went down the stairs and into the kitchen to find something to appease his growling stomach.

His head was in the fridge when he heard Law's voice behind him. "Do you always roam strange houses in the middle of the night? Because that's a good way to get yourself shot."

"Is that a threat?" He hadn't turned from the refrigerator, only doing so after he'd found the makings for some sandwiches. When he went to the table he noted that Law did indeed have his gun next to him.

"Fact."

Cole tried his best to look unimpressed, although it was hard in the face of Law and his gun. While Cole found Marcus intimidating, it had been tempered by Marcus's obvious attraction to him. There was none of that with Law. There was only suspicion, bordering on what looked like complete distaste. And it would be foolish to think that Law didn't know about his past. "Want a sandwich?"

"I'm good." But Law made no move to leave the table. And even though Cole had completely lost his appetite, he still made the sandwich and forced himself to eat it. "By the way, there's a shelter on King Street."

He glanced up at Law, his stomach roiling. "I don't need a shelter." But it came out as more of a question, because maybe it was a suggestion Law was giving him.

Law stared at him steadily. "It's ours. We run it. So if you know anyone in trouble, send them there."

Cole wanted to say something sarcastic, but nothing came out. Instead, he nodded, put his dish in the dishwasher and went upstairs to Marcus, his head spinning.

What would Cole have done if that had been available for him back in the day? Things might've been so different. And even though he didn't like to dwell on the past, the whole thing made him sad for time lost. He climbed into bed next to Marcus, unable to bite back a sob that would wake Marcus as he thought about that and the kind way Marcus treated him. Marcus had given him back his dignity.

For a long time, Cole hadn't felt like he was worth anything, but after he'd explained that to Marcus, Marcus murmured to him that he was wrong. "You were never not worth it. You're a survivor, in my book."

"Guess you'd know about that."

Marcus ran a hand through Cole's hair. "You weren't the only one who was broken."

18

THINGS DIDN'T GET ANY BETTER WITH LAW OVER THE NEXT FEW days. The nightly scene repeated itself, and even though Cole knew that Law was running shelters, it didn't mean that Cole was any more comfortable around him.

But he was dealing with it, because he wasn't seeing Law during the day. But that changed one morning when he went out to the side carport area, which had to be passed through before anyone could get to the garage, to get some air. He figured he'd be okay there—he was half-hidden by pillars, with a good view of the front and backyards. Law's bike was also parked underneath it.

Cole took a deep breath of fresh air and almost choked when Law said, "What the fuck are you doing out here?"

"Dammit, you scared the hell out of me." Cole shook his head, his pulse jolted. Law didn't say anything, just crossed his arms, waiting for an answer to his question.

Cole sighed. "I'm going stir-crazy."

"Did you tell anyone you were coming outside? I'm guessing no, since none of them would've let you."

Cole stared straight ahead, refusing to look at Law. Wanting to punch him, actually, which would be a very bad idea since his partners were giving Cole a free ride. But he couldn't stop his mouth. "You and Marcus are a lot alike."

"Somehow I'm thinking that's not entirely a compliment, even if you are screwing him," Law said casually.

Cole turned to face Law—the guy hadn't moved, but he also hadn't blinked. "A real goddamned Dick—maybe you could put that on your Phoenix, Inc. business cards."

"Yes," Law agreed, much in the same way Marcus had done. "But fiercely fucking loyal to people I love."

It was both a warning and a promise.

"I'm not out to hurt them," Cole protested.

"You're a lot more like me and Marcus than you realize."

Yeah, Cole had noticed that too and still wasn't sure how he felt about it. "And?"

"Just an observation."

Christ. He turned his back and glanced around. Heard a soft chuckle behind him. He asked "what?" over his shoulder.

"I may be an asshole, but you trust me."

"How's that?"

"You turned your back on me."

"Asshole," Cole muttered. He stomped away from Law and his stupid grin. He didn't want to think about the fact that he might have a chance to become a part of their tight-knit extended family—or what that meant. Or if it only extended to when and if he and Marcus were together, or until the job was over, and then what? Right back to where he started. Alone.

Which sucked...but would suck worse after having this family and then losing it. Which is why he was pissed he let himself connect in the first place.

As he turned away, something about Law's bike caught his

eye. He'd only been permitted to touch it once when it was something beyond Law's ability to fix on his own—and with Law breathing down his goddamn neck the entire time—but now he zeroed in on something. Maybe it was the angle and maybe it was a stray leaf or some shit like that, or hell, maybe Law rigged his own bike to explode but...

He edged closer. Bent a little, used his penlight and saw the wires.

He didn't hear Law come up behind him, and he jumped a little at Law's voice when he asked, "What's wrong?"

"When was the last time you rode this?" Cole asked.

"Late last night."

Jesus. Either it happened overnight or Law had been playing Russian roulette and neither option was a very good one. He pointed. Law looked over his shoulder toward the bomb nestled under metal and swore loudly.

"Fuck me." Without looking at him, Law said, "Go inside and grab Marcus for me, will you?"

Cole didn't wait—he moved quickly, going inside and calling for Marcus as he hit the door. It was probably something in his voice that made all three men—Marcus, Styx and Paolo—assemble in the front hallway. "Law's outside. There's a bomb strapped to his bike."

Marcus moved by him, clapping a hand on his shoulder before he walked out the door. "Are you okay?"

"Just help Law" was all Cole told him. He watched both Marcus and Styx head to the driveway. Paolo pulled him inside the house a bit and closed the front door.

"It's all right, Cole," Paolo assured him. And Cole knew that the bomb wasn't the issue.

The two men could easily defuse that, but the question

remained in his mind—what if Law hadn't noticed it this morning? Or would he have?

"This is getting on my goddamned nerves," Law announced after the bomb was defused and lying on the kitchen table in front of them. "How is this guy just disappearing? He's as good as..."

He trailed off as he stared at Styx and pointed accusingly.

"Fuck me," Styx said slowly.

"Later," Law said. "We're dealing with a spook. And shit's about to get ugly."

"My stalker's a spy?" Cole repeated. "That's really fucking bad."

Marcus nodded. "It's like having the king of stalkers."

Cole groaned, dropped his head into his hands.

"It's okay, Cole," Paolo reassured him.

"It's not. I keep putting you directly in danger," Cole practically shouted.

"Calm down, princess," Law said.

Styx stopped behind Law. "That's usually my nickname for you."

Law rolled his eyes. "I'll save the glass slippers for later."

"Cole, this is actually a good thing, okay?" Styx tried to assure him further.

But Cole knew it wasn't. Still, he nodded, then turned and left, going out the back— which was admittedly stupid, and Marcus caught up with him anyway.

He felt Marcus's strong hand on his shoulder, heard the man's demand of "turn around or I'll carry you back inside."

"Fuck off." He turned, shrugging Marcus's hand off of him.

"If I ever got one of them hurt or killed...if I ever took them away from one another...I'd never forgive myself. Assholes, all of you. I'm not taking on that shit."

He stormed back inside feeling trapped as hell. Because he was.

19

"HE'S GOING TO RUN—I FEEL IT," PAOLO SAID.

Marcus agreed, which was why he wasn't taking his eyes off the camera, which showed Cole lying on the bed, staring at the ceiling. "I can practically hear the wheels in his head turning."

"But this shit? It's not fair to him," Styx countered.

"Now you think of that?" Law asked.

"I wasn't thinking. I was in the fix-it mode," Styx said.

"We all were," Marcus agreed. Getting Cole to forgive him was one thing. Trying it now would only seem a transparent way to keep him in the house. "I fucked this up."

"We all did," Paolo told them all. "But he's safe. There is no great way to handle it. But letting our guards down now..."

He trailed off. They all knew the statistics, what happened when the stalkers' prey got tired of running or thought they could go it alone. This was the critical time.

"How could none of us have noticed him?" Law asked. "That bomb had to be wired. It wouldn't have taken long, but fuck, are we going soft?"

Styx considered that quietly for a long moment. "I think we

need to check the perimeter alarms. Now. Marcus, you okay to stay with Cole?"

There was no place Marcus would rather be at the moment. But when he went into the room they were sharing, he found Cole the most agitated he'd ever seen him. He was practically vibrating with anger and pain, and yes, he'd pulled out a bag but was too wound up to even pack.

Marcus approached him carefully. "Cole..."

Cole whirled on him. "You know...I get it, okay? I understand all of it. I'm not some stupid street kid. But all this trust shit, acting like you've accepted me—it's got to stop. Because we can just treat this like what it is. I don't expect anything from any of you once this is all done. I'm not even paying you, and still you're all putting your lives on the line for me. Do you know how that makes me feel?"

Marcus was still reeling from the sucker punch of Cole's statement that he didn't expect anything from anyone. "What if I want you to expect something from me?"

"Why? So I'll stay in line, listen to you and stay in this house forever?"

"No, that's not why." He stopped. Cole wasn't going to believe that. Instead, Marcus sat down on the side of the bed that was empty and then lay down next to Cole. "I'm so pissed at you. Until you, dammit—you, not your case, but you—I've never wanted to protect someone more in my life for the most selfish reason. I want you here for me."

There was still so much they didn't know, still more trusting left to do and bridges to cross. But this...this was the start.

Cole was literally on him, straddling him, arms on either side of Marcus's head as he bent forward. He didn't say anything. Didn't have to. The look in his eyes... Yeah, Marcus felt a wave of relief wash over him, especially when Cole brought his mouth down on Marcus's. And it went from that to *I need you naked now* in about five seconds. Hands scrabbled. Clothes flew.

And then they heard the applause.

Cole started and Marcus sighed, muttered some curses then yelled, "Turn that fucking camera off. Assholes."

A wolf whistle sailed up the stairs. "Too bad—we were going to sell it and call it *The Men of Phoenix, Inc.—Part One.*"

He glanced at Cole, and for a second he worried that Cole might be sensitive about what was most definitely a joke. But Cole was smiling. "Think they really turned the camera off?"

"With those guys, who knows?"

Cole shrugged and stripped all the way out of his jeans. When they didn't hear anything at all from downstairs, he said, "I kind of miss the applause."

Marcus laughed and flipped Cole to his back, palming his cock. Cole arched up into his hand. "Yeah, Marcus. Hurry."

"We need lube."

At his words, the door opened and a bottle of lube sailed through the air. Marcus caught it and looked back as he heard raucous laughter. Paolo stuck his head in, his hand over his eyes. "I'm not looking—just apologizing for these two. They're children. Given their advanced ages, you'd think they'd have more sense."

The laughing stopped, and even with his eyes covered, Paolo smirked, the expression of a man who knew exactly what he was doing. "Gotta run."

And he meant that—literally. In seconds, there was the sound of heavy feet. Some muffled thumps. Paolo would give them a good chase, but in the end Styx and Law would win.

. . .

Cole was listening, his eyes wide when he heard a bark of a command, followed by sounds of the struggle. Then there was the muffled sound of a slap on bare skin and a low cry that was so full of need. Marcus watched Cole's face carefully all the while.

"Don't worry. He does that on purpose." Cole stared at him. "They hit him?"

"Spanking. That's what it sounds like to me. And he likes that a lot."

Cole raised his brows. He was still hard and he shifted under Marcus. "You do that?"

Marcus trapped him, moving his face inches from Cole's. "You want to lie across my lap, or over the bed? Or on all fours and let me take my hand to your ass?"

As if to punctuate the question, Paolo's moans drifted over them after a series of thumps, and it assured Cole that yes, that was exactly what he wanted. Sure, a couple of johns had given him a few swats while fucking him, but that had been back when he'd still answered to Jax—the name he'd been born with. Even then, he hadn't been into that scene, and neither were his clients. And now he'd shed that name along with his former profession. "I don't want to decide how it happens though. I want you to make that decision."

Marcus didn't pause or make him feel stupid. Instead, he hauled Cole up and over his lap. Cole found his hard cock pressed against Marcus's thigh. He felt vulnerable and nervous and awkward, and then Marcus's palm hit his ass, followed by a second and a third slap, and then he lost himself inside the hot, dirty burn. He wasn't aware of how loud he was—how hard he'd come—until he came to on his belly on the bed, with Marcus rubbing his back. "Baby, that was…"

Cole blinked. He'd never come like that. "Shit. Was I loud?"

Marcus nodded. "So are they. They don't care, Cole. If there's one thing they understand, it's sex. Good sex."

Cole nodded. He never really thought of himself as having a lot of inhibitions but he'd been wrong.

When he'd been hooking, he'd been bold and not given a shit. Cole was actually surprisingly innocent. Having Marcus be involved in so many first times, ones he never thought he'd have back, was probably the greatest gift he'd gotten.

20

PAOLO

STYX ALMOST CAUGHT HIM ON THE WAY TO THE THIRD FLOOR—
Paolo had been cornered, unable to go down, so his only hope
of escape was the third-floor attic, where he could lock
himself in.

Or let himself get caught. Eventually. But first, the chase.
Because it was fun to throw taunts about "old men huffing and
puffing to keep up" as he skirted them. As Law's hand nearly
closed on his biceps, Paolo ducked and rolled out of the narrow
hallway and into one of the bedrooms, locking the door behind
him. He leaned his full body weight against it, wondering if
they'd actually kick the door down while they had other people
staying in the house.

He could only hope.

A minute passed. Then two. And then he turned his head
right and found Law. Inside the room. With him.

"How the fuck?" Paolo asked and Law shrugged.

"Old men have their secrets." He moved to Paolo, who stayed pressed to the door, and reached overhead to unlock the deadbolt. He smiled. Then he flipped Paolo onto his back on the floor and was straddling him when Styx walked in carrying the two camera monitors. He set them up on the night table as Law guided him to the bed on all fours. Half mounted him and whispered, "You keep your eye on those screens. You can't not look, can't not keep the house safe, no matter what else is happening, right?"

Ah fuck. He opened his mouth to protest, to apologize, to something, but he couldn't. Not when Law's hand began reaching under his shirt, playing with his nipple. Not when Law yanked his jeans down and swatted his bare ass hard. Once, twice, and he groaned, loud enough for the neighbors to hear.

"How many, Paolo?" Styx asked. "Two," he managed.

"Outside?"

His gaze fixed on the screens, put close together so he could sweep them with one look. "Clear."

"Really?" Styx sounded amused. "Look again, because the old man swears he sees something."

"Ah, okay... Mrs. Sellers. Walking..." *Slap.* "Her." *Slap.* "Dog." *Slap.*

"Good," Law crooned, and Styx, the taskmaster, asked, "How many?" and Paolo had no fucking idea, and told Styx exactly that. Which earned him more slaps. Which he didn't count. He cursed them both, which earned him more hot, delicious, burning slaps from Law's hand until he sagged and felt the salted tears burning his cheeks. But he kept his eyes on the camera because, hell, he hadn't meant to forget that.

And then Law was kissing his cheeks and Paolo was murmuring "sorry" about distracting them, and Law was holding him and telling him that they counted on him for good distractions.

"I've got this, Paolo. I can watch the perimeters and your show at the same time." Styx's deep voice was softer now, his hand running through Paolo's hair, and, fuck, they loved him so goddamned much that sometimes it hurt to think about.

Law was guiding him to his back now, spreading his legs, fingering his hole. His abused ass cheeks burned against the comforter, but man, it felt so good too. Law kissed him hard and fast, his tongue dancing along Paolo's. Paolo wrapped his legs around Law's back—the guy was already naked.

"Need lube, babe," Law told him.

"No—want to feel the burn."

"Oh no," Styx told him. "Not when we have our anniversary coming up."

Paolo started for a second, looked between the men. Because their anniversary of committing to one another wasn't the one Styx was talking about. Couldn't be because...

"He doesn't remember," Styx said.

"I'm sure he remembers—maybe not the exact month it first happened but..." Law said, and then it clicked and Paolo's cheeks burned. "Yeah, that's right, Paolo. It's time again. Once a year, because the anticipation's almost as good as the real thing."

He pictured himself trapped between Styx and Law in that cabin, trapped in the snow, trapped by Styx's past...impaled on both men's cocks as they took him simultaneously.

"Think he'll pass out again when he comes?" Styx mused, caressed Paolo's hair again, jerking it a little, forcing Paolo to look at him.

Law pushed inside of him, and then Styx angled himself so

Paolo could suck his cock. Paolo's ass and mouth were full, held helplessly hostage by them, his body vibrating in pleasure.

"Jesus, he's beautiful," Law said to Styx, and, really, that was all it goddamned took to make him come, right then and there. He was so easy for these men...but the best part was that was exactly how they liked him.

21

MARCUS WENT DOWNSTAIRS FIRST, TELLING COLE HE WAS GOING to turn the camera back on. Cole showered and then went downstairs as well, a tiny bit relieved to only have to face Paolo, who was alone in the kitchen, the camera to his right as he flipped absently through a magazine.

"Hey. Sorry about all that," Paolo said, not looking the least bit sorry, but rather flushed and well fucked.

Cole could understand why Paolo had chosen not to sit. Cole joined him, leaning against the counter on the opposite end. "It's all right."

"Don't worry. We watched the perimeter cameras the whole time. We know what it's like to mix business with pleasure."

"That must've been…interesting."

Paolo laughed and Cole felt his face redden. "*Interesting*'s not the word for it."

"Mind if I grab some food?"

"I've actually got some pasta on the stove. Should be ready in about…" at that moment, the timer started buzzing, "…now." Paolo didn't wait for Cole to answer. Instead, he got out bowls and plates and forks and napkins, but he only spooned enough for him and Cole. "The others are outside, working on some flaws in the perimeter cameras. They wanted to wait until it was dark."

Cole dug into the spaghetti appreciatively. It was delicious, and he told Paolo so. And then he ate three helpings, as did Paolo. And Paolo had already put on more water to boil to make more spaghetti for the three men who still hadn't come inside.

"Why don't we go and sit on the couch? More comfortable than these chairs."

Cole nodded and followed Paolo into the living room, all the while wondering how Paolo knew what he and Marcus had done. He was pretty sure Marcus wouldn't tell Paolo, and he'd figured that Paolo wouldn't think twice about him standing.

Paolo sank into the couch cushions with a sigh and a small grimace. Cole lowered himself gingerly as Paolo said, "I just figured by the way you were walking. Takes one to know one, you know?"

"That was the first time I..." He blurted that out, then trailed off because what the hell? But Paolo just nodded understandingly. "We're pretty open about things around here, as you can tell. Doesn't mean you have to be, but you should feel free to ask questions. I know what you've done in your past, but I also know that that doesn't always give you the kind of experience necessary for you to really have a good time in bed."

There was no judgment in his tone. In fact, Paolo's eyes were a little bit heavy. And he just looked blissed-out. It was exactly how Cole felt, so for a while the two men just sat there, content with their full bellies and their own thoughts, waiting for their men to come back inside.

Finally, Cole said, "They're lying in wait for him, aren't they?"

Paolo smiled sheepishly. "I told them you were gonna figure it out. They told me a lie by omission was the best way to go."

"You think there's a chance the guy will come back tonight?"

"No way. I think the bomb on Law's bike was a warning. He wants us to know that he can get to us. I figure he waited to see when, not if we found it."

"You think he was there, watching us when we found it?"

"When you found it," Paolo corrected with a slight wince. "And yes, I do. And hell, having them wait outside tonight? It's a long shot, but worth it. We've got to outthink him. Because whoever this guy is, he's good."

"He's got to be, because I know how good all of you are."

"Those three are former Special Forces. I'm just a cop, but I've picked up a lot on the street and from them. But hell, they obviously still baby me."

"Does that bother you?"

"Sometimes. But I finally learned that all I have to do is smile and nod and pretend to agree and then do whatever the fuck I want anyway. They get mad, then they get even. What usually happens is pretty much what you heard before, so how bad is that? It's a win-win." Paolo laughed and Cole joined him. "I know you want to help, but really the best thing for you to do is what we tell you. If we're worrying about you, we can't do our jobs effectively. If we know you're safe, then we can go balls to the wall."

"I know some self-defense. It's pretty basic, so I'd definitely like to learn more." Cole stared down at his hands. "I'd like to learn to shoot too. I didn't tell Marcus that yet but..."

"It's not a bad idea at all. We can definitely go to the range. I can see what you've got, defensewise, and I can show you some more moves. I'm sure the other three will add to it. We've all got our secret maneuvers that get us through."

Cole thought back to some of his own secret maneuvers that he'd had to use over the years, not so much on customers but on other street kids like himself. They'd thought they could roll the "pretty boy" and take his money, his clothes, his dignity. He'd fought for all of that, and he'd always won.

He'd keep winning. No way was he letting that stalker take anything else from him.

Marcus could be back in the jungle for all the darkness and the heat and the buzzing insects. He and Styx and Law had all agreed this was probably a useless exercise, but it still had to be done. The guy looking for Cole was getting agitated, and agitated people tended to make stupid mistakes, no matter how well trained they were. That was why the military and then the CIA tried to beat emotion out of its people. The more emotion you felt, the less in control you truly were.

Based on how he felt about Cole, Marcus could really and truly understand that.

Just then, another car came down the street and pulled into the neighboring driveway. A man and a woman got out of a minivan and went into the house, their hands clasping on the last third of their way up their own front walk. That was nice to see. Made him think of Cole waiting inside for him and how much he'd allowed Marcus in earlier that evening. Marcus felt at once undeserving and extremely grateful.

"Dead out here," Law said into Marcus's earpiece. Indeed, it was just after two in the morning. If this guy was going to show, this was the dead time to do so.

Earlier, Law had bitched about how he wished he'd left his bike out on purpose and had thought to put a bomb of his own on there, because then this whole thing would be done. The fact that Law had left his bike outside instead of locked in the garage told Marcus how much this case must be affecting him.

He didn't know much about Law's past, but he knew it hadn't been great. The fact that he avoided Cole way more than the others did told the rest of the story. His past had to mirror Cole's in some way.

Marcus's gut tightened whenever he thought about what Cole had been through. He had to push that out of his mind in order to keep functioning, because if he let himself get wrapped up in that, there'd be nothing left for this surveillance, this job. "I'll stay out until sunup. You guys take a break," he murmured into his mic to Styx and Law.

"I'll stay out here with you, Marcus. I know Law's got a lead he wants to follow. It involves a lot of computer work, and Paolo was going to help him with that." Styx was maybe a hundred yards away from him, but they could have been on opposite sides of some jungle, based on how well they were camouflaged. But this was how they were trained, and it normally got results. Granted, Law did this kind of surveillance better than any of them, although he'd be damned if he'd ever admit it.

"I'll keep my earpiece in. Call out if you need a break," Law told them. For tonight, he'd put his bike in the garage, but they'd put out their recycling cans in hopes those would lure the stalker to plant another bomb.

Marcus knew what would really put the guy over the edge, and he'd been reluctant to even bring it up. He knew the rest of them were thinking the same thing. It would take one night out with all of them and Cole, with each of them showing him some kind of affection, and the guy would go fucking ballistic.

Of course Cole would be all over that plan. Which is, of course, why Marcus hadn't suggested it. Because it was dangerous. Because it could backfire so easily. Would be so much better if he could just hunt this jackass down, sniff him out like the dog he was and fix it so he could never do this to anyone again. Because there was no way this was his first time stalking. No, the stalker had this down pat. A textbook case.

He started at that thought.

A textbook case. His mind went into overdrive, and in a quiet voice he began talking to Styx.

22

LAW

LAW PUNCHED SOME KEYS ON THE COMPUTER FROM HIS SEAT AT the kitchen table, with a bowl of spaghetti next to him. Because, even at three in the morning, he'd never say no to Paolo's pasta.

He'd also watched Paolo and Cole spar for a while, while his searches were running. They'd been at it a while, judging by how much both men were sweating and panting. Law had to give Cole credit—the kid, who wasn't a kid, was damn tough. And Paolo was taking this very seriously, teaching him some of the tricks that Law and Styx had taught him, even as recently as two or three weeks ago.

He stared at the screen as he shoveled in a few mouthfuls of spaghetti twirled on his fork. He still had access to many databases he normally wouldn't have. Styx did as well, and so did Marcus, but they were monitored more closely because of their former CIA connections. As former Delta Force, Law was so classified he could often fly under the radar, as contradictory as that sounded.

Right now he was searching prisons for recent release cases over the past year. Stalkers generally were not put in jail for a very long time. If they violated restraining orders, typically they'd only receive a slap on the wrist. Any type of violence or vandalism might net them bit of actual prison time, but any stalker who was truly serving a sentence...well, it meant they'd followed through and killed their prey.

Now, Law listened to Marcus talking to Styx through their shared earpiece, Marcus finally voicing his concerns about just how textbook this case was. Law couldn't agree more. The problem with prison was that these guys were forced to meet with psychiatrists and sometimes those very doctors who tried to help them actually allowed the men to see deeper into their psychoses by explaining what was wrong with them, teaching them new ways to be better and more proficient at their stalking.

He'd gotten a few hits and he printed out some pages because he'd follow up on those later. Now, he entered in a code that allowed him to bypass several layers of security so he could search military prisons. The biggest problem was that none of these guys would've been sent to prison for stalking. That would've been something in addition to whatever they were serving time for, something that people might not have even noticed.

He shifted in his chair, his hip aching. And whenever his hip hurt... "Gonna storm, guys," he said into the earpiece. "Lightning and thunder coming your way in less than two minutes."

In about thirty seconds, Styx and Marcus were in the kitchen as lightning illuminated the sky behind them. Ten seconds later, a boom of thunder sounded. Something tightened in Law's gut, and he went into the closet, grabbed his military-issue drab green poncho. He pulled it over his head and walked out into the same storm he just pulled Styx and Marcus in from.

23

Marcus watched Law literally disappear into the night. "I'll go out there with him."

Styx shook his head. "We'll keep an eye on him on the monitor. I'll watch him and you watch the perimeter, okay? We both need some food anyway."

"Does he do that often?" Marcus asked, for the moment keeping an eye on both Law and the perimeter while Styx dished out the pasta. It was still warm, since Paolo'd heated it for Law just a bit ago.

Styx sat next to him, and they ate in silence for a few minutes until Styx said, "He's really good out in storms, if that's what you're asking. But he's been able to predict the weather for a really long time. Let's just say it's in his bones."

Marcus had served with men who had a lot of really quirky traits, and he believed in that shit, because those quirks had tended to save his ass. Suddenly, he felt Cole's hands on his shoulders. He glanced quickly up to see Cole's flushed face and disheveled appearance. "Were you boxing or something?"

"I was teaching him a few moves," Paolo said, looking similarly sweaty and disheveled. "We were sparring, Marcus. Get your mind out of the gutter."

Cole laughed, and that actually made Marcus's gut untwist a bit. There'd been so much worry, making it hard to enjoy just being with Cole. But seeing Cole relaxed and comfortable made him mouth a silent "thanks" in Paolo's direction. Paolo gave a brief nod back, then looked over Styx's shoulder. Outside the storm really began to rage.

About an hour later, after they'd eaten more and remained talking at the table, the lightning stopped. Law came in from the darkness, soaked to the bone, and Styx sent Cole and Marcus upstairs to grab some sleep.

When Cole climbed into bed next to Marcus, he mentioned that he thought Law had been abused.

"I didn't ask or anything, some things you just know," Cole added quickly.

Marcus wrapped himself tightly around Cole, wishing Cole didn't have to know as much as he did.

It was still pouring when Cole woke. In the short time he'd been staying here, it'd turned into some kind of routine—he'd wake around four in the morning, stroll downstairs to the kitchen to get something to eat and Law would come in with his weapon and watch Cole and the monitors simultaneously. The first time it happened was two nights before the bike incident, but Cole wasn't sure what would happen tonight.

Last he'd seen, Law was dripping wet and Styx was helping him take off his clothes. He'd assumed that Law wouldn't come down tonight.

"You come down here because you're worried about me."

Cole turned from the refrigerator to see Law, who was

already sitting in the kitchen chair without Cole having ever heard him come into the room. And although what Law said hadn't occurred to Cole, at least not on any conscious level, now that it was out there he couldn't deny the truth. Still, he wouldn't give Law the entire satisfaction. "Maybe."

"I wait down here for the same reason." Law's smirk was a little twisted but his eyes held the sincerity that Cole had probably missed all these times. "It's a gift, you know, being able to spot our kind."

Cole gripped the back of the kitchen chair tightly, his eyes clouded for a moment with tears he wouldn't let fall, and his throat felt tight. "At first, I thought..."

"I know," Law said softly. "You remind me of someone from my past. It's not a good someone, but it's just a physical resemblance, and I had to get over it. But the recognizing our kind—that had nothing to do with it. Sorry if you thought I was judging you."

All this time, Cole had thought that Law was the toughest of all of them, the most hard-assed, hard-shelled. In reality, he was the softest, and therefore he needed that rough exterior to keep out the hurt of the world.

And Cole opened his mouth to say something, maybe all of that or maybe not, but nothing came out except a small sob. He tried to choke it back, but it didn't matter. Because Law was next to him, his arm around him, letting Cole bury his face in his shoulder. It was probably one of the only nonsexual times he could remember hugging another man, and that probably made him cry a little bit harder. Because although he'd told Marcus this and Marcus had been good about everything, there was just something about sharing it with somebody who'd obviously been there in some way or another.

And when Cole pulled back a little, he saw that Law's eyes were wet with tears as well. "Sorry, I didn't mean—"

"'S'okay, Cole. I needed that too. We try not to let it overwhelm us, but sometimes..." Law smiled. "You must be hungry —make your sandwich."

Cole watched Law move to the other side of the table a little stiffly, almost with a slight limp. "Are you okay?"

For a long moment, he was pretty sure Law wasn't going to answer him, but then finally he said, "The rain, the snow... childhood injuries."

"Anything I can get you?"

"Four Advil. Top cabinet." Law pointed and Cole got him the tablets, some milk, as Law requested, and then made them both sandwiches. They ate in comfortable silence, listening as the rain began to slam against the house again.

Cole wondered if Law would go back out there, or if he'd had enough of the storm. "Do you think he's out there?"

"I do. This is a game to him. We just have to learn how to play it better." Law sounded confident, but he looked troubled.

"Do you think it's someone from my past?"

"Unfortunately, yeah, it's gotta be. Guys like us, we tend to attract people we don't even realize are attracted to us." Law motioned to the bread. "Can you make me another one? That was good."

And Cole did. And the two men sat there together, and Cole listened to Law's story. At first, it appeared that Law was going to leave some parts out, but he didn't, and when Cole heard the whole thing, he understood why Law had thought about not sharing his whole background. But it seemed to be as cathartic for Law as it was for Cole.

"It sounds like you really found the right guys. I was pretty envious of you three, because I never thought I'd find one guy and here you had two who couldn't take their eyes off of you."

Law grinned. "You've definitely got a guy who can't take his eyes off you."

"You think?"

"Sometimes it's okay to let your guard down, Cole. If you don't, you'll miss the best things in life."

"When did you realize how alike we were?"

"The first day I met you at the garage," Law admitted. "Come on, let's get you back to Marcus before he gets even more worried."

"He's sleeping."

Law rolled his eyes. "He's already checked on you five times."

Indeed, when Cole went back into his room, Marcus was awake, flipping through TV channels absently.

"Sorry—didn't mean to worry you," Cole said.

The smile on Marcus's face let Cole know that Marcus was well aware of his nightly trips downstairs and his interactions with Law. "Glad you guys got things figured out."

"Yeah, me too." He wanted to ask Marcus about all the stuff they had to figure out, and he thought about things that he'd left unsaid. Was it time to talk about it? Because as much as he wanted to, something in his gut told him that it wouldn't go over well. Ever. And maybe, just maybe, it was something he could keep hidden for long enough that it wouldn't matter.

24

SETH

SETH WATCHED THE MAN NOW KNOWN AS COLE WALK THROUGH the hospital with the tall man

who should be dead. Seth had put the bomb inside Law's bike as a test for Cole. He'd told himself that Cole was only with these men because they were holding him, forcing him, the way Cole's former boss had forced him to sell himself.

Until Seth had freed him.

Until Cole had left without warning. Now that, Seth hadn't anticipated. Cole had looked at him so warmly, and he'd figured that Cole was on his wavelength. That they were soul mates. That Cole would understand that he was supposed to go home and wait while Seth did what he had to. Which was, of course, take revenge on the man who had hurt Cole in the first place, the one who'd forced him to get naked and sell his body to strange men for money, the one who'd forced him to steal.

He'd known that Cole needed to be cleansed. Seth had experience in that. And now that he had Cole back in his line of sight, Seth realized it was a losing battle. That Cole had already been lost to him, too far gone. Perhaps he'd misinterpreted Cole's signals.

All he knew for sure was that the new, young boy in the hospital bed was waiting for Seth's help. And even though Cole would be of no use to him, that didn't mean he would be allowed to live. He would cleanse Cole the only way he knew how, and then he would help the new boy.

He would never let either of them go. He'd been told his next steps, and he always listened to his dreams.

They'd started three days after his last tour, occurring only at night, which was when— and why—Seth had stopped sleeping. He'd been discharged from the hospital for minor contusions after a land mine exploded in front of him, totaling the unlucky supply truck and all the men who had been riding in it. His ears still rang, a persistent, tinny buzz he couldn't rid himself of. At times it drove him crazy enough that he would box his own ears in so the pain would override the constant, deafening sound.

Yes, the Army had let him go. They taught him things, made him a machine and then they expected him to forget all that knowledge. But he knew he could be needed at any time, had to keep himself strong, able to do what he'd been doing in the sandbox. And he had been asked back, to the CIA, for a special joint task force that he'd served on for three years. The ringing in his ears never stopped. It was only made better when he visited his boys. He fed them. Gave them love. And then he absolved them and was able to go back to work in peace. But when he no longer had work to go back to, he'd realized he had a higher mission to complete.

He'd still visited his boys, always new ones, but he needed a sign—an angel—and when he'd happened upon Cole, the light had shined and he'd known he'd finally gotten his wish. The incessant ringing in his ears had ceased for just a second when Cole smiled. That couldn't be coincidence.

But his angel had been called Jax, not Cole, and he'd felt deceived when he discovered that, but he'd been willing to forgive Cole. Until Cole betrayed him. He'd often watched the garage where Cole worked, to keep an eye on him. Normally, he'd see Cole talking with other mechanics, but that one day in particular, when the man looked him up and down and Cole hadn't walked away, Seth knew something had happened. Cole had been left alone for too long. He thought he could fix it, until those other meddling men got in the way.

Now, he'd show them just how serious *his* mission really was.

25

IT WAS AFTER MIDNIGHT, FOUR NIGHTS LATER, WHEN LAW CALLED his name. Cole looked up from the book he'd been attempting to read, but really he was too damn restless to do much at all. "What's up?"

Marcus and Styx were outside doing their surveillance again. Paolo was monitoring the perimeter cameras in case they missed anything, but after night after night of the same silence, it was pretty obvious that the guy knew they were on to him.

"I've got to go to the hospital," Law told him now.

"Are you all right?" Cole asked, looking him up and down.

Law gave a tight smile. "No, I'm not all right at all. But I'm not the one who's hurt."

And even without any more information, Cole was up putting his boots on, grabbing his jacket. Law was talking into his earpiece, telling Marcus he was going to take Cole with him. Marcus must've not objected, which relieved Cole. Because he wanted to do something for Marcus, for all of them, and sitting around being protected just made him feel guiltier. He knew

Marcus would worry...but he also knew Marcus would understand. And so Cole followed Law out the back.

"I called a cab to come pick us up on the next block so no one would follow us. The patient we're going to see doesn't need any more problems than he already has," Law explained.

Cole's stomach twisted, because he had some idea of what Law was talking about. Marcus and then Law had both told him that they all did community outreach work, mainly centering on kids in need. Having been one of those kids in need, he could only imagine what was waiting for them at the hospital.

When the cab pulled up outside the ER doors, Cole asked, "Do you know this kid?"

"I didn't say it was a kid."

"You didn't have to." Cole got out of the cab and shut the door. Law paid, and together they walked through the open doors that sucked them into the noisy waiting room.

"I don't know him. One of the social workers called me in. From what she said, he's in pretty bad shape but he won't talk about what happened. Says he fell down some stairs. He's seventeen, emancipated from his parents. No job on record."

Cole knew what that meant. The kid had to be doing something to earn cash. "Drugs?"

"Social worker said he wasn't high and the police didn't find any drugs on him." Law wanted to say something else—Cole could tell—and then Law told him, "You don't have to come in, Cole. You really don't. I know this is a lot to throw at you, and really I just needed somebody to be here for me, for afterwards. I know that sounds pretty selfish."

Cole stared up at Law, surprised that the big man would admit that. "I don't think that's selfish at all." And then he followed Law into the private room.

Initially the bed was blocked by two policemen in suits. Detectives. They were talking to the kid in the bed, and Cole could hear the muffled angry curses the boy was throwing at them.

"It's important that you talk to us, Julian," one of the detectives was saying. "It's not the first time Kingston's done this, and it's not going to be the last. He murdered the last one. Is that how you want to end up?"

Cole winced at the question, mainly because he knew it would have zero effect on the boy, or at least the opposite one the detectives were going for.

"Maybe if you left me alone with him for a while," Cole suggested softly to Law, who looked at him like that was simultaneously the best and worst idea ever. "I wouldn't offer if I didn't think I'd be okay."

"I always think I'm going to be okay at this stage," Law admitted. Cole knew he was probably right, but he was already here and he was the best one to help Julian deal with this. He let Law talk to the detectives, who obviously knew him. They looked at Cole, and one of them looked familiar, maybe from the garage or the diner or around town. He figured that Phoenix, Inc. had let the police know about his stalker as well.

Finally, he was alone with Julian. "Great, another fucking do-gooder. Here for college credit?"

Cole laughed—he couldn't help it. "I'm pretty much the farthest thing from a college boy or a do-gooder that you can get."

"You're friends with someone who knows the police." In Julian's world, that was as good as being the police. Then again, Julian didn't look or seem all that comfortable in the world he'd been thrown into. In fact, Cole's radar pegged him as a beginner, which meant he could stop him before he got really stuck.

"Does he beat you when you don't bring home enough money or is it just whenever he feels like it?" Cole asked bluntly. Julian started but quickly recovered, saying "fuck you" under his breath.

"No thanks. I gave that up a couple years ago. Five years was enough time to waste." Julian was looking at him suspiciously, like he didn't know if Cole was just putting on an act or if he could really be trusted. So Cole continued, "I worked the streets for maybe two years. Buddy of mine, as much as I could be buddies with anyone, invited me to come work with this guy who ran a service. He said it would be safer, that it paid better. And hell, I was tired of giving blowjobs in back alleys. It was fucking cold in New York."

"Did that guy beat you?"

"No, he didn't. He used me just the same. But I got rolled on the streets quite a few times before I decided to start fighting back. Taught myself some self-defense moves by watching a class at the Y. If I was gonna be alone with johns, locked in a motel room, I was gonna know how to get them off of me."

Julian looked a lot smaller and younger than seventeen lying in the hospital bed, his face bruised and his ego shot. "I've only been working for two months."

"Runaway?"

"Aren't we all?" Julian shrugged then said, "I'm not going back. I can't go back. They kicked me out."

"I've got someplace you can go."

"With you?"

"It's not a place I run. But the guy I came in here with? He was like you and me once. He and his friend both. Now they give money to open shelters—safe places. And they find ways to give you jobs, ones that actually make you some money. But the shelters? They're designed for you to live there while you work and save money. There's free food. Free medical care. From what Law told me, a lot of the guys who come in at fourteen and fifteen and sixteen actually stay on and do a lot of the counseling." Cole drew a deep breath then. "Julian? Fuck, I hate to lecture. I'm the last one who should be—I stayed in the life for seven years altogether. I'll have to live with that for the rest of my goddamned life. It's hell on relationships. It's ruined me in ways you can't even imagine. I might look fine. I might sound fine. But I'm not fine. You need to get out."

Julian's eyes were downcast for a few seconds after Cole's speech, and then he admitted, "He said he owned me, that he'd kill me if I try to get away."

"They all say that," Law drawled. Both Cole and Julian looked at him in surprise. "No one ever hears me coming."

"And what are you going to do to ensure that this guy's not going to come after me?"

Julian wasn't a stupid kid. He had an education—that was apparent just by the way he talked. That probably made life on the streets worse for him.

Law smiled at Julian's question and then said, "You tell me where this guy lives. I'm going to pay him a visit. He's not going to bother you or anyone again because he's not going to stay in this town."

There was something so menacing in the way Law spoke, and yet Julian looked like a hundred-pound weight had been taken off his shoulders. Because Law's anger was so obviously not directed at him and definitely an emotion anyone would want behind them.

"Hey, Cole? Are you and he...?" Julian motioned between Cole and Law. Cole shook his head no. "But there's someone. Finally."

"And he knows? I mean, about your past."

"He knows. And it's okay." Both men looked at the door where Styx and Marcus were coming into the room.

"I know which one it is," Julian said quietly. "The look on your face says it all."

"You'll get that one day."

"You really believe that?"

"I'm living fucking proof."

26

THE NEXT MORNING, MARCUS GOT A PHONE CALL FROM CLINT. He'd been expecting some new information, as Clint had hinted, but nothing like what he'd gotten.

First, Clint told him that the Marine in question, their best lead for Cole's stalker, had an airtight alibi. He'd been KIA two months earlier. And then Clint dropped another bombshell on him that left him reeling.

"Are you sure?" Marcus heard the tightness in his own voice, could feel his chest pounding as he spoke to his friend from the CIA.

"I am," Clint said quietly. "And I'm sorry."

"Nothing to be sorry about. I just wish I knew this sooner."

"Marcus, if you've fallen for this guy…"

"I haven't," Marcus said firmly.

"Which one of us are you trying to convince?" Clint asked.

"Come on, Clint—am I supposed to make it work with the guy who sells himself and then steals from the man he worked for? We're not talking about a small amount of money."

"So the stealing part bothers you more than the sex?"

"Everything goddamned bothers me about this." Cole had withheld important information...information that could possibly help them narrow down the profile of the stalker.

"I know. But come on—that's not an easy thing to admit. I might've admitted to jail first."

But it was tugging at all of Marcus's old anger buttons—if Cole stole money from a wealthy guy—who then accused him of stealing from his clients too...

Shit.

He listened as Clint gave him a little bit more information so Marcus could run his own search, which he did after he hung up. And he was right back again to that first relationship, when he discovered how used he'd been then. For two years, he'd thought the man he loved had loved him back. In reality, that man had taken his money, his gifts and given them away to other men. It was only after overhearing the guy on the phone telling one of the many men he'd slept with that "Marcus is very easy to use, and he's loaded. This is the perfect arrangement for me," that he knew what'd been going on.

Cole might not know for sure that Marcus had money...but he'd seen the beach house and, hell, he probably recognized what he considered to be Marcus's type.

Well, Marcus thought he'd recognized Cole's type as well. But he'd let himself be taken in. Now, it was time for both of them to pay the price.

Marcus called his name, and Cole got a chill from Marcus's tone. Marcus's expression was worse. Fuck, it stopped Cole cold. It was worse than it had been the first time Marcus had looked at him in the diner. Suspicion was now mixed with such anger.

Unfortunately, Cole knew all too well what'd brought it on. He'd been waiting for it to be revealed, all the while praying it wouldn't be. He'd been second-guessing his decision to leave that part of his life and his past out, arguing with himself that he was allowed his secrets. That what he was hiding didn't have anything to do with his current situation.

Unfortunately, in Marcus's eyes, it had everything to do with what was happening between them.

Nothing stays hidden forever.

Cole hadn't given Marcus or the others his real name—they assumed he'd never hidden it because he'd had no reason to. But he had several friends he'd made when he'd spent that bit of time in prison, unable to make bail, and those contacts were helpful when it came to starting over the way he had. Obviously, those documents had been worth their weight in gold, since several ex-CIA guys plus a former cop hadn't been able to ferret them out.

Not until Marcus had decided to dig. Or maybe...

Maybe your stalker's known the entire time.

"Hey," Cole started hesitantly. Marcus was coming at him fast, but Cole didn't shrink away, met his fury head on. Because he was done with being afraid, done with being judged... done with all this shit. He'd never asked for promises and he'd never given any.

"Why didn't you share the fact that you had a record?" Marcus demanded. "I didn't think it was important."

"Really? The fact that you did time in jail for theft isn't important to share with me... because of the case? Or on any level?"

Cole straightened, his anger rising quickly, as it always did when the old accusations reared their ugly heads. "I was in prison, not jail. I didn't steal anything. And don't tell me they don't put innocent people in prison."

"I never said that...but I figured you'd be honest with me. Your fucking life's on the line. Mine too, along with Styx's and Law's and Paolo's."

"Don't. Don't you dare do that to me. My prison time has nothing to do with this stalking."

"Maybe it's someone who knew you in prison."

"And maybe it's some random person who I met in a grocery store!" Cole shouted. "You said it yourself—there's no rhyme or reason to this sometimes. And I don't know you well enough to tell you everything about my life."

Marcus's eyes flashed.

Cole pointed. "Tell me about your life, Marcus. You've told me some really specific shit—I'm the master at knowing when someone's only telling me a slice of their life. But the difference is, I don't find the need to pry into it. Secrets are secrets for a reason."

"You don't deserve to hear about more of my life. It's not putting you in danger. And what you did..." Marcus was so angry he couldn't even finish, Cole realized, and his own anger and humiliation and self-doubt slammed into him head on.

"What I did? Last I looked, I fucking survived. We've had this discussion."

"No we didn't. We didn't go over how you stole from your johns and your boss, or the part where you went to jail for it."

"I didn't fucking steal anything," Cole said through clenched teeth.

"Right. But the charges were dropped so you didn't have to prove it, one way or the other. You also conveniently forgot to mention that your name isn't really Cole."

"Yeah, it is. I don't answer to any other name these days."

"Using a false ID is illegal. With your record—"

"Fuck you. Like you're so worried about me? Like this isn't just some attempt to back away from me as quickly as you goddamn can? Basically, Marcus, you've been looking for an out the whole time. I've tried to prove to you that I'm not that guy, whoever he was. But you're always going to look at me like that."

"Can you blame me? You did the same thing to me that he did. You used me and you lied."

Cole's suspicions were confirmed—he didn't need any further details. "I didn't ask for anything from you. You know that. I didn't want to accept this help."

"But you did."

Cole's face felt hot from shame. He'd never thought anyone could make him feel like that again, least of all somebody he was falling in love with. Yet, here he was. And so he charged at Marcus like a raging bull, and Marcus's rage met his head on. All he could do was take the pain and anger out on Marcus and let Marcus take it out on him. He heard fists hitting flesh and they were both grunting, but there was none of that sexual energy that always happened when they were play sparring. No, this was all too real and it could get ugly fast.

Uglier, anyway. But maybe this was the best way to let things end, the way Cole knew they would from the start. Because if they ended on a slightly sweet note, or with Marcus pitying him, he'd never be able to live with himself. No, this way was better, with painful bruises and some drawn blood and cursing, until strong hands tore him away.

Styx was holding on to Marcus, who was staring at Cole with a coldness in his eyes that Cole had actually never seen. It spoke of his pain and made everything just that much worse, made him sick and dizzy, to the point where suddenly the hands that had been holding him back were holding him up.

"Fuck you for not trusting me," Marcus told him.

"Your reaction is exactly why I never trusted you to begin with," Cole heard himself say, and maybe it was the truth or maybe it wasn't, but he couldn't have stopped himself from saying it. And that was all it took for Marcus to yank himself out of Styx's arms and walk out the door.

Cole jerked away from what turned out to be Paolo's grasp, half noticing that Law wasn't anywhere to be seen, and resisted the urge to follow Marcus. What could he say? That he was sorry? In his estimation, words were never enough. In this case nothing would be.

27

PAOLO

PAOLO ONLY CAUGHT THE TAIL END OF THE ARGUMENT, BUT THAT was enough. The last thing he heard was Cole telling Marcus that he didn't believe his stalker was from his time in prison. "Yeah, I made tons of friends in prison who were released at exactly the same time."

Cole rolled his eyes. "I wasn't in long enough to be in with the general pop. That wouldn't have gone over well."

Paolo knew a young, handsome guy like Cole would've been bait. He could fight, but eventually...

Paolo shook his head to shake the what-ifs. He'd seen more than his share of young kids pay the price of "should've known better".

"You're a million miles away." Styx's hands were on his shoulders.

"Back at the precinct," Paolo offered, looking up at the man he'd hated on sight, on principle. Although that thin line between love and hate had really been thin as hell.

"I heard it got rough here today."

"Marcus called you?"

"Cole did. He felt like shit that he didn't tell us."

"And what did you tell him?"

"I told him we'd talk about it, but that he knows we don't judge. Honestly, I don't think it's anybody that he met during that time. He wasn't in long enough, and since we cleared that Marine and his boss from the agency... Hell, it could be anybody. It could be somebody he met on the street last week."

Paolo nodded, because he knew that. But he couldn't shake the feeling that he was missing something—a big something. He hadn't realized how tense he was, not until Styx's strong hands kneaded his shoulders. He practically groaned as the knots began to loosen. "I was thinking..."

"Always dangerous," Styx said seriously.

Paolo ignored him. "What if we were slightly off track? We know this guy is good. What if he's a dropout?"

"That makes him even more dangerous."

A lot of the men who didn't make the cut for the Academy, whether police or FBI or CIA—or even military—were still as highly trained. Sometimes they got all the way through training before the cracks showed through. Not everybody failed their psych test at the beginning. "It's still a long shot, and it still leaves us a hell of a lot of guys to look at."

"It's a shorter list than agents and retirees." Styx was rubbing his hands through Paolo's hair, and, damn, the men had good hands. He knew it too because there was a slight chuckle in his voice when he said, "I'll get right on that after I finish here. We could start with a sweep of police in the precinct where Cole was arrested."

"Yeah, I think that'd be best," Paolo mumbled, dropping his

head a little lower to give Styx access. This scalp massage felt incredible.

Marcus walked away, out of the house and probably out of Cole's life for good. And while Cole really couldn't blame him, a big part of him did.

It was only when he'd gone upstairs and the anger began to subside slightly that he realized they'd had an audience, no doubt an unwilling one, but hell, it was their house. And he didn't want to turn around to face Paolo or Law—especially not Law, because even though Law knew better than the others, well, Law probably would've told him not to lie in the first place.

He'd let Marcus down, and Law and the others. And so he'd called Styx and confessed because that had been easier than a face-to-face. Now, he stood in the middle of the room he'd been staying in with Marcus, trying not to look at the bed or Marcus's bags, not sure if he was supposed to leave.

Just as suddenly as he began to think about that, he was surrounded by the three large men, their stances surprisingly comforting, especially when Cole got up the nerve to look in their faces and found compassion. Compassion but not pity.

"I'll call Marcus back. Or maybe you should," Paolo told him.

And just like that, the anger welled up again. "Did you not hear him?"

"I did," Paolo said evenly. "But I still think that you calling him back would mean a hell of a lot."

He opened his mouth to say something like "you've got to be fucking kidding me", but then he heard Law say instead, "I've got this, Paolo."

And when Cole looked at Law, he noted that the guy looked as haunted as Cole felt.

"Law…" Styx said with a gentleness in his voice that tugged at Cole.

But Law waved Styx off, motioned for Cole to follow him. Once they were out of Styx's earshot (if that were even possible), he said, "Is that everything? All the cards on the table?"

"It is."

Law nodded. "You guys said some pretty terrible things to each other."

All Cole could do was shrug, although the pain of those words felt like a knife in his chest. In fact, he was finding it a little hard to breathe and he just didn't want anyone to have to deal with one of his panic attacks. Not now, after such a freaking scene. Not after they just found out that he'd been arrested, accused of stealing. "I didn't steal from anybody. Ever. But he doesn't believe me. He doesn't want to believe me."

"Breathe, Cole." Law's words were more like instructions, and it helped Cole to tamp it down, the same way he had for Marcus. Except that made him think of Marcus, which made him sad, and mad all over again. Which made the panic worse. For a little while everything kind of blanked out, and he supposed it was better that way. He couldn't talk or deal with any of this shit, and maybe now everybody would just leave him alone.

But…no such luck. Because when he blinked and realized that he could breathe and see again, Law was still sitting there, concerned but yet unmoved. "Give Marcus a chance."

"I get that he's a friend, but—"

Law interrupted. "I lost ten years I could've had with Styx. It wasn't my fault, but if there was something I could've done to stop him from disappearing, I would've."

"I'm not you. Marcus isn't Styx. We're not..."

"Bullshit. You're both so far gone you can't see straight."

"Sometimes that's not enough. Don't you get it? Just because you got lucky doesn't mean all of us do." He heard the coldness of his own voice, saw Law recoil, almost as if he'd been slapped. But Cole was too far gone to care. He didn't have strategies to get through this shit. His strategy had always been to run, and so far that had worked for him. It kept him from making connections that would hurt him, like these had. And it had stopped him from hurting people, the way he had Marcus...and now Law.

"What I get is that Marcus didn't grow up like us. Not even close. Did you ever stop to think that maybe he's been hurt by guys like us, but not us? Because I'm damn well sure that you've been hurt by guys like Marcus before."

How Law managed to sound so calm amazed Cole. "I never had something like this with any of the guys I fucked for money," he said bluntly. "You have no idea how much I opened myself up to him."

"It's scary. It's always going to be scary until you two put it all out on the table. You need to know that you can get to a place where neither one of you is going to run...at least not very far or for very long."

"What you went through...how do you not let it bleed into everything you do?" Cole asked.

Law considered that for a long moment. "I've had longer to deal with it, for one thing. Jesus, Cole, you're still right on top of what happened to you—I'm surprised you have as much perspective as you do. Also...it does bleed into things. I almost lost the best things that ever happened to me because I didn't want to deal with any of it. But they won't let me get away with anything."

Cole wanted Marcus to not let him get away with things...to not yell at him for everything. "Marcus isn't like that."

Law smiled. "I didn't say that I didn't do anything for them. That's what love is. It's give and take. And I get it. With your dad, it was mostly give on your part. You need to learn balance." With that, Law got up and said, "I'll call Marcus, okay? Go try to get some rest and get your head on straight."

Cole didn't know what else to say, so he did what Law asked of him.

Marcus got the call when he was three blocks from the house. He knew he shouldn't be away from the men for any length of time, for all of their safety, no matter how angry he was. But he didn't stop driving as he took the call.

A black-ops job. A high-paying one, just like the many he'd turned down countless times since retiring. He wasn't sure why he was considering it this time, because he knew better. He knew that those kinds of jobs were certainly not an escape from real life. But somehow, he felt like the pain of that past might somehow override the pain he felt right now.

"I'll think about it and I'll get back to you in twenty-four," he told the man on the other end of the line.

"We'd love to have you, Marcus. You're always high up on our list."

Marcus supposed that should make him feel good, but it was exactly the opposite. And as he turned the truck around to head back to the house, Law called him.

"I'm going to be pulling into the driveway in five," he told Law.

And when he did pull in, he wasn't surprised to find Law covering him with a shotgun. He hadn't felt the stalker's presence, not before he left, not when he was gone and certainly not now. Which was odd.

And when he walked with Law back into the house, all he said was, "This is supposed to be a job, not drama."

Law snorted. "Welcome to my world."

28

STYX RAN A HAND THROUGH PAOLO'S HAIR, MASSAGING AND caressing. Law watched the scene, an outsider looking in, if only for the moment. And he was strangely okay with that, with watching something he'd never thought he'd have but somehow did. There was something comforting about knowing Paolo and Styx genuinely loved each other, that they weren't just doing it for him. Some guys might've wanted the opposite, might've been jealous as hell. But not him.

It had been hard enough thinking, at one point, that he'd have to choose between those two men. He knew now that he couldn't have made that choice...and he was thankful he didn't have to. This love was simply right, but that didn't mean it was easy. It was just that, with love, you didn't mind making the effort.

The two men sitting in the kitchen definitely made the effort with him, and he knew he hadn't been easy to live with these past weeks. Or...ever, really.

He also knew that Styx was watching him without watching him, even right now while all his concentration seemed to be focused on Paolo. Indeed, at one point he looked out and caught Law's eye. Smiled. It was an invitation to join them, but there was no pressure. Law gave a slight nod. He would join, but sometimes just watching was also nice.

He'd thought about going upstairs to talk to Cole again, numerous times, to make sure he and Marcus didn't butt heads immediately. But Marcus had gone to a bedroom on the first floor instead. He and Cole both needed a cooling-off period. In truth, Law did as well. It hadn't been easy to hear Marcus confront Cole about his past, even though Law had long suspected that Cole was holding something back. It was inevitable, and no one could ever be sure what another person's personal shame might be.

The fact that Cole had kept the secret about being accused of stealing and the subsequent time spent in jail wasn't a surprise. The fact that Cole had talked to Marcus so candidly about his time on the streets? That had been a surprise to Law, who'd never been able to open up to anyone that easily—not after such a short period of time.

He heard Marcus come into the room behind him, but he didn't turn around, choosing instead to focus on the two men who would no doubt be naked in the next five minutes.

"You all right?" he asked Marcus.

"You're really going to concentrate on me when you have them right in front of you?" Marcus asked without a hint of judgment or irony in his tone.

Law turned to him. "They'll keep." And then he got up and motioned for Marcus to follow him outside. They both had their weapons on them, and they stayed close to the porch, scanning the area out of habit. They'd also made sure they were positioned behind some of the taller chairs and the columns so they wouldn't be easy targets.

"I don't think he's here," Marcus said, and no, Law didn't get that feeling either. And he'd been watched enough times during his Delta Force days to know.

"You and Cole had a hell of a fight." Marcus grimaced. "Sorry about that."

"You don't have to apologize to me. I've been there."

"As the secret keeper, or the one pissed at the secrets?"

"Both," Law admitted. "But you can't let him hide forever."

"Just until his urge to hit me passes."

"I don't think that's going to be anytime soon."

Marcus sighed. "You're not going to tell me how wrong I am?"

"Can't tell you how to feel," Law said easily. "But how do you feel?"

"Like I was motherfucking lied to."

"Well, you were."

"We're risking our lives for this. I mean, he sees that and still he did nothing," Marcus fumed.

"True. We all have things we don't want to admit."

"Don't do that, Law."

"What? Be logical? I know—it throws people sometimes," he said easily. "And are you really mad that he didn't tell you because of the case? Or are you mad he didn't tell you for other reasons?"

"Fuck you and your logic."

"I didn't have to tell Greg much—he knew. But telling Damon and Styx...well, that took a while. And it changed a lot for me. You've got to give Cole time, Marcus. He was thrown into all of this, and he feels responsible. Sometimes having secrets is a very necessary thing for survival. And Cole's a survivor. So am I, all right?"

Marcus stared at him. "I realize that you'd been in a certain kind of hell yourself at one point, which means you understand him. And I'm trying, Law, but even if I do understand... he's pissed at me."

Law snorted. "Well of course he's pissed. You *are* kind of a dick."

29

COLE HAD GONE UP TO THE ATTIC AFTER HE AND MARCUS argued, where he could see the comings and goings of the whole neighborhood. Law went outside and then Marcus pulled into the driveway. No one came up here to him, which was good. He was still so tightly wound it might take a week before the tension bled off.

He supposed he could use the gym the guys had set up in their basement. But that meant dealing with Marcus. And while he was far from a coward, he didn't want to go another round of "you use rich men for a living".

But inevitably—maybe even surprisingly—Marcus did come up, much sooner than Cole expected. And he was carrying a plate of Paolo's pasta like a peace offering.

"I want to throw it at your head, but I'm too hungry," Cole admitted.

Marcus gave a small, rueful smile and handed it to him. "I figured."

"Which part?"

"Both."

Cole ate as Marcus looked out the window. He was almost done when Marcus, without turning back around, said, "I've had some bad experiences. They've colored my judgment."

"Yeah well, me too," Cole said. He put the plate down and moved to sit on the edge of the double bed.

Marcus did turn to him finally. "Rich-boy problems, I guess."

"Definitely." He paused. "I get it, okay? A lot of guys I worked with are exactly the kind of guys you're talking about. I'm not one of them, but hell, I could tell you forever and that wouldn't mean anything. I guess showing you's the only way to prove anything to you, but if you're thinking I'm going to be stealing money from your wallet every five minutes…"

"I don't think that, Cole," Marcus said quietly. "It's just…I loved this guy. He hurt me, worse than I'd ever thought I could be hurt."

Cole's face hardened, and for a second, Marcus wasn't sure why. And then he realized… Cole was upset for him.

Cole was also jealous.

"Who was he?" Cole demanded. "And when?"

Marcus sat on the bed next to him. "I'd really rather not talk about him."

"Why? You've still got a thing for him."

"No. If I saw him tomorrow, I'd say hi, but I wouldn't feel anything—not love, not hate. Just, whatever. But at the time…it colored everything. Made me look at anyone and everyone who came into my life from that point forward differently."

Cole nodded. "I can see that. I had the same issues. Still do. Most of the rich guys I met were assholes." He paused. "By the way, you acted like an asshole today. Like you did when I first met you. And I figured you had money. Well, not for sure, but I mean…"

"I'm an asshole?"

"Yeah. But in a good way. At least now."

Marcus shook his head. "You sure know how to compliment a guy."

Cole laughed.

"So..."

"Yeah." Cole sighed. "Look...after this, I always assumed..."

"That what? We'd be done?"

"Yeah."

"Is that what you want?"

"I didn't want to want anything, Marcus. I don't want to want anything I can't have. Hurts too much."

"Suppose you could have your wish?"

"You first."

Marcus nodded. "I'd want to keep doing this. I know we've got to face the real world soon enough. But I feel like we've gone past dating."

"We jumped right into living together."

Marcus snorted but then noticed the expression on Cole's face. "What's wrong?"

"Sorry, nothing. Just...I don't know if I've still got a job. I could go back to the apartment, but after that guy's been there..."

"No, you're not going back there," Marcus told him. "No way."

"Then what?"

"You're coming home with me."

"Is that an order?"

"Cole, come on..."

"What? Mooch until I get on my feet? And have you worry the whole time?"

"I wouldn't."

Cole stared at him. "I would."

"I think we both have to get over ourselves."

"You first."

Marcus sighed. "I got a call about a job. Like the work I used to do."

"The work that gave you nightmares?" Cole asked quietly, but without judgment.

"Yeah. And I was considering it. And not just because we were fighting. But maybe...maybe one good mission to end on would erase the bad."

Cole reached up and ran a hand through Marcus's hair. "I don't want you to go, but I'd understand if you had to. Why you'd have to. Maybe you could put some of those old ghosts to rest."

"Do you think that's a good idea?"

Cole considered that for a long moment. "Is it going to do more good for others than for you? Because I'll tell you, Marcus, you don't owe anybody anything. You paid your dues. The only thing left to prove is how good of an agent you are, and as far as I'm concerned, as far as the men who offered you this job are concerned, you already are. Sometimes, all it takes is for us to forgive ourselves. I know that's easier said than done. But if you can try to do that, to forgive yourself for me..."

As Cole's voice broke, something inside of Marcus did too, but it wasn't a bad thing. No, it was the entire wall that had been put up, crumbling, letting out all of the bad feelings he'd had from those missions, from that failed mission. Cole's words were things he hadn't allowed himself to even think about dealing with, let alone say out loud.

"Thank you," he managed.

"I didn't do anything."

"Ah hell, Cole...you did everything. You are everything."

Cole wrapped around him, hugged him hard. "I'm sorry I lied to you, Marcus. It's just...look, everything I did was for survival. I can't justify it. But selling myself as an escort to those rich guys? It made me feel more like a whore than when I was working the street. I don't know why. And then I went to fucking prison for something I didn't do. On the street, I got hit, but I never got accused of trying to use rich guys. But I don't want that to be a hang-up between us. And I think I made it one."

"We'll figure it out, Cole," Marcus assured him.

30

JULIAN'S FACE LIT UP WHEN HE SAW COLE AND LAW COME INTO the room. "Hey, I hope you guys brought food from the outside, because this shit? It's terrible." He pointed at the JELL-O on his tray and then waved his hand over a mess that looked like gravy and possibly mashed potatoes.

Law held up a bag of greasy fast food, which immediately brought a smile to Julian's lips. He handed it over, and Julian began to rip into the food like he hadn't eaten in weeks. Which, Cole thought, he probably hadn't.

As if reading his mind, Law put a light hand on Cole's shoulder and squeezed gently. The message was, no doubt, something along the lines of *Don't worry—we'll fix this. We'll keep him safe.*

"Have the doctors told you when you'll be discharged?" Law asked when Julian's feeding frenzy had slowed a touch.

Julian nodded, said, "The doctor said in two days. And that cool social worker you sent said he'd escort me there personally," before shoving a handful of fries dipped in ketchup into his mouth.

Cole froze. "What social worker?"

If he noticed Cole's worry, Julian didn't show it. "Some guy —can't remember his name but he wore one of those white coats. He said he knows Law and that I'd be fine from now on."

Law just nodded, gave Cole a hard look and left the room for a few long moments.

When he came back, the doctor was behind him. "Just a quick check-in," the doctor told them.

"We'll step out. Julian, we'll be right outside," Law told him. When they got into the hallway, Law didn't wait. "There's no male social worker that visited Cole. There are no male social workers who work at this hospital right now."

"What do we do now?" Cole asked, forcing down the now all too familiar panic. Surprisingly, it happened easily, this time replaced by a war of anger and determination. "I won't let that freak get near Julian."

Law was texting, no doubt to Styx or Paolo or even Marcus. "We can go at this a couple of ways. One of us—meaning me, Styx, Paolo or Marcus—can stay here with him. Be the surprise wild card when that 'social worker' returns. Plant a false release date."

"No way—this guy's too smart for that. He scouts before he makes his move. If he knows one of you guys is around, he'll never do it. But if I'm there..."

Law's lips clamped together, but he didn't say anything.

Cole said quietly, "I realize this guy wants to kill me. I realize that Julian is probably my replacement. But I also know that making myself vulnerable might be the only way to end this."

Law winced at his choice of words, and to be honest, Cole did as well, but he stood firm. "I'll call Marcus and the others.

Talk with them. We'll have to be here, scattered through the hospital. We are *all* gonna have to up our game for this one."

"Do we tell Julian?"

"I'd want to know." Cole's words reverberated through Marcus. He put a hand on the younger man's neck, rubbed and forced himself not to rethink his decision to let Cole be in the room with Julian when the stalker was in close proximity. It was such a risky thing. Such a stupid thing. But they'd run out of choices, beyond Marcus and Cole running away and hiding. And neither man ran any longer—that was one thing they'd agreed on.

Marcus had picked Cole up and taken him back to the house to talk to the others, leaving Law to watch Julian. They figured that the guy was going to be looking out for anything unusual, so they decided to wait until tomorrow in order to execute the plan fully. That is, if they all agreed.

Marcus glanced at Paolo, nodded, and Paolo said, "Julian's not you. He's got no experience at all. He won't be able to fake it if he sees this guy again, and that will give away the whole plan. We need the stalker to feel as comfortable as possible. Like he's won. You can explain this all to Julian afterwards. Or maybe, if we're lucky, Julian never has to know about it at all."

Cole swallowed hard, and Marcus pulled him in for a hug, murmured, "If I could've saved you from knowing this..." He trailed off, because it was obvious what he would've done, how he would've handled it. And it had nothing to do with Cole not being strong enough. It was about how, once you'd seen too much, there was no way to unsee it. No way to erase it from your brain. No way to get rid of the pain completely.

The garage was heated, the door leading into the kitchen

was propped open and the main door on the garage was locked. Unless the man after him was a mouse, Cole couldn't be safer, but that didn't stop Marcus from watching him like a hawk. Which, of course, drove him fucking nuts.

"I can't work like this," Cole complained. He needed to get himself centered on this plan, and he needed to make sure all the panic was gone. Which meant he had to turn to doing something that could take his mind off things. As much as he wanted that thing to be Marcus, he needed some space from him to turn off the worry. "Walk away and do something else."

Marcus rolled his eyes. "Fine. I'll be in the next room."

When Marcus finally left, Cole muttered to himself, because Marcus no doubt still had the camera trained on him. But it still allowed him that space and pretty soon he began to lose himself in taking apart the old bike that Styx had rescued long ago on a mission. The bike was from the 60s, Army issue, although over the years people had tried to make modifications. What they tried to add didn't match what the Army had created, and Cole was a master at making sure the new and the old blended together perfectly. This wasn't a one- day job or even a week's job. No, this was a project and something he'd needed desperately.

He owed Styx for so many things, but for this…

Hours passed. Someone switched on the light in the garage for him, and he wasn't sure who because he never looked up. His hands were full of grease and so was his shirt. At times he'd look and find a bottle of water or some food next to him and he'd halfheartedly eat or drink as he rewired and reworked portions of the bike.

He heard the three men laughing in the living room, heard Paolo's snort, Styx's reprimand for God knew what. Law's booming laugh was missing, which meant he was still with

Julian, and then there was the rumble of Marcus's voice that went straight down his spine and to his dick.

He put the wrench down, and thought about how much Marcus affected him. How easy it would be to just go into the room and assimilate with them at this moment. And they'd let him—Marcus would pull him down onto the couch next to him and they would keep laughing and joking and pretend that they weren't here for any other reason but a job.

But you are *a job.*

And that reminder was like cold water on him. He shivered, and realized how cold it had become suddenly. Which is odd because there was heat earlier. He was about to stand and check the thermostat when he caught the sound of a rush of wind. He turned and realized that the garage door had been cracked slightly.

"What the—"

He didn't get the last word out when a hand closed over the front of his neck and his mouth. A hard body pulling his to it. The grasp was unyielding. Terrifying. The voice in his ear was even more so. "Good to see you again. I've really missed you, Jax."

Cole knew that voice...but from where? He didn't have time to process more.

Under the man's hand, he whimpered, realized that they were moving, going through a panel that had been cut into the back of the garage. And then they stopped moving, and the man's hand went down the front of his pants and gripped his cock that was flaccid from fear and stroked it. Cole half sobbed under the man's hand as he felt himself get hard.

Simple biology. That's all it was.

The terror ran through him like a goddamn river of rage and pain, and finally his body unlocked. He managed to move.

Kick. He elbowed the body holding him but the grip never wavered in its strength. The hand moved faster, and the voice said, "I'm going to open you with my cock, the way I wanted to when we first met. I've been planning. Gonna make it so good for you. Trust me, baby."

Trust me, baby. He continued struggling, managed to cry out for Marcus, but it sounded so low to his own ears, and the man continued to stroke him and then suddenly he was alone. He turned around, scared, confused, and saw Marcus there and Styx and Paolo running in the direction of the woods. Marcus was leading him inside the house. Sitting him down. Checking him over.

Cole wanted to tell him to calm the fuck down. But he realized he must be in shock because he couldn't get a goddamn word out. Marcus was talking to him and it was like he was seeing the man through a haze of water. His ears were clogged. He couldn't move his body.

It was then he realized that the man who'd gripped him had drugged him.

"Cole, it's okay. Styx's got something that's going to get the shit out of your system fast. It's the reason you can't move. You're going to be fine. You're safe."

Cole desperately wanted to ask if they'd caught him, but he knew that they hadn't. Because Marcus would've said that first thing.

31

Even though Cole was rousing, thanks to the meds Styx had on hand, Marcus insisted they call an ambulance. As the EMTs checked Cole out under Marcus's and Styx's watchful gaze, Paolo talked to the police.

"He'll be okay," the EMT was saying. "We could take him in for observation, but you reversed the drug's effects, and all the hospital would do is keep him under observation."

"With this asshole still out there, I want him close," Styx said tightly, and Marcus agreed, even though the guilt of how this happened washed over him.

At that moment, Cole moved his lips, and Marcus moved closer to catch the soft words.

"I know who he is."

That was the only good thing to come out of this, and it had been far too close a call for Marcus to be anything resembling happy. "Good, Cole. Let's get you through this and then you can tell us everything you remember," Marcus soothed him, fighting the urge to ask questions.

And then Cole asked, "Julian?"

Marcus understood immediately. "We think this guy followed you and Law to the hospital—or he traced you. But Law's at the hospital with Julian. He's fine."

Marcus's gut churned. If Julian was the guy's "new" target, then he was no doubt ready to get rid of Cole, who'd be considered the "old" one.

"Thanks," Cole whispered.

He kept contact with Cole, putting his hands on Cole's shoulders, telling him, "This won't happen again. Know that."

Cole nodded.

"Good. The EMTs are going to take your vitals again. Rest. When you're ready, we'll go over everything."

Cole squeezed his hand and fell off to sleep again. Marcus and Styx watched his breathing go from shallow to normal within a half an hour. The EMTs stayed longer than they normally would've, thanks to their connection with the Phoenix, Inc. men. The police were also going over things with Paolo.

Marcus stood from where he'd been semikneeling by the couch and walked a few steps away as the realization of what almost happened hit him like a Mack fucking Truck.

"Marcus, we'll get him." Styx touched his shoulder.

Marcus glanced over to where Cole was lying on the couch, the EMTs checking his pressure. He looked handsome and oh-so vulnerable, especially with the bruise marks circling both forearms and wrists.

Those marks made Marcus flinch. "He was close. So goddamned close, and I should've stayed close. Sat in the fucking garage with him."

"He told you to go. He's a grown man. He was in our house," Styx said.

"We can't protect him."

"Yes we can. And we will. We got to him in time," Styx reasoned.

"I'm done hiding," Cole said from behind them, his voice a little woozy. "This isn't anyone's fault. Marcus, please…"

Marcus's fists tightened as he listened to Cole's reasoning. Then he turned and went to Cole, knelt by the couch. "I want to protect you."

"You have—you do." Cole swallowed, licked his lips. Marcus held up water for him, and Cole drank greedily. "Thanks. Better."

"Good. Just rest, okay?"

"I need you to stop blaming yourself. Blame that asshole, but not yourself."

Marcus took the fact that Cole was cursing as a good sign. He'd rather have Cole pissed than scared, if forced to choose between the two.

Slowly, agonizingly so, the feeling came back into Cole's extremities, allowing him to move. First it was his fingers that began to tingle and then it was his toes, and then a whole hand and an arm and then his calves. Everything started pins and needles from the outside and worked its way in. The ability to wiggle his toes was infinitely far more comfortable than it should be. When he could stand, he did, with Marcus at his side, even as Marcus insisted he should still be lying down, resting.

"Fuck that. No," Cole told him.

"Stubborn," Marcus muttered, but he couldn't hold back his smile. "How about if I lie down next to you?"

"How about you fuck me?" At Cole's words, there was a deep, almost primal rumble that came from Marcus's chest. He was well aware that Styx, Law and Paolo could hear every word, and he didn't care. It almost made him bolder.

"Jesus, Cole..."

"I need you to touch me," Cole demanded. "I won't go to sleep—not real, nondrugged sleep—with that memory. I need you to fix that. And you can."

He stared into Marcus's eyes, willing the man to agree...to still want him. Because that was as damned important as needing the bad shit washed away.

After a long moment, Marcus's eyes remained gentle with concern but his voice was low and growly when he spoke. "I'll take you to bed. And I'll touch you. Fuck you. I'll give you what you need, and you will not fucking panic with me." It was a command. It was exactly what Cole needed, what he needed to hear.

All he could do was nod, and Marcus growled, "Good. Let's go."

Cole let Marcus guide him, a hand on his lower back. There was no explanation to the other men, and they simply watched with semibemused expressions. They'd keep guard tonight, and that would allow Cole to let go.

Once they were alone in the room where he'd always felt safest, Marcus steered him to the bed. Cole's legs hit the bed, but he stayed standing, mainly because Marcus was pretty much holding him up.

"Take your shirt off," Marcus told him, and he did, the sluggish feeling that'd been dogging him for hours was finally wearing off. His skin was tingling, but for different reasons. "Jeans next. Strip for me."

Cole shimmied out of his jeans and boxer briefs, kicking

them away, slightly unsteadily. But Marcus's hands were holding him firmly. He leaned his head back against Marcus's chest, wanting the man to throw him down and take him.

And he might've said that last part out loud.

"You're mistaken if you think you're the one giving the orders," Marcus said, a bit of actual laughter in his tone. "Shower first."

He let Marcus take him into the bathroom, where it was Marcus's turn to strip and then put them both under the warm spray. The water drummed a thousand soft drops on his skin, soothing him. Marcus held him close, moved the washcloth along Cole's back, rubbing it in lazy circles. Then he washed Cole's hair, touching the pressure points along his scalp to try to relax him. All the while, the suds were washing away the scent of the man who'd violated him, maybe more than he'd ever been, until all he could smell was fresh soap and Marcus.

Marcus, who was now spending time between Cole's legs, gently but firmly cleaning Cole's cock, then getting on his knees and sucking it down his throat. Cole grabbed the towel bar for support as everything bad started to recede, replaced by white-hot jolts of pleasure.

"Marcus, I'm going to..."

Marcus let Cole slide out of his mouth. "Don't" was his simple command before his tongue played in the slit on the head of Cole's cock. Cole stiffened and groaned as Marcus pushed his tongue hard, like he was fucking that little hole and if Cole held the towel bar any tighter he'd pull it off the goddamned wall.

"Now you can come," Marcus said, his tone lazy, right before he took Cole in his mouth again. At that, Cole came immediately, shooting down Marcus's throat, unable to look away as Marcus swallowed everything, and continued sucking...so much so that Cole was semihard again once they got out of the shower.

Marcus wrapped him in a towel and practically carried him to the bed. He pushed Cole to sit, then toweled him off, making sure to wrap a dry towel around his shoulders when he was done.

And then he took Cole's arm gently and stared at it. For a second, Cole almost lost it, felt the familiar panic threaten.

Marcus stared at him, shook his head. "What did I say?"

"Not to panic."

"Then don't. I'm going to fix this, then fuck you deaf, blind and dumb." With that, Marcus began to kiss the bracelet of bruises circling various parts of Marcus's wrists and forearms. Immediately, Cole forgot the panic, mesmerized by the new, pleasurable pain of Marcus sucking his skin hard, suckling the bruises, circling them, covering them with his marks until all Cole could see were the hickeys that his lover gave him.

Once again, Marcus was taking away the bad the best way he knew how.

Cole let himself be manipulated by Marcus's strong arms. The sucking and biting were lulling him into a near trance, and by the time he blinked, Marcus had him lying on his belly, cheek on the pillow, so comfortable he could fall asleep.

Except for his stiff cock that definitely needed attention. "Marcus, I need..."

"I know, baby. Trust me, I know."

Cole's breath caught as Marcus's cock slid back and forth between his ass cheeks. He was so full of need, his body started to shake as if it would come apart. Like the blood was traveling too fast in his veins, his heart pounding in his ears, an out-of-control jetliner careening across the sky.

"Marcus!" Because even if this wasn't going to be a forever

thing, at this moment all Cole wanted was to pretend that it was. Marcus had erased all those nameless, faceless men he'd fucked along the way and now he was asking Marcus to erase his attack.

Marcus gripped his hips, pulled him to his knees and entered him. Cole barely managed to get up onto his elbows before Marcus's weight pushed him balls deep into Cole's ass. He froze, letting himself adjust to Marcus's girth and length, both of which were considerable. And then Marcus's hand was reaching around, palming Cole's cock...taking away the other man's touch. Making him fly. Soar.

He was aware he was yelling, but it didn't matter. Marcus rocked them back and forth, faster and faster as Cole stared at the bracelets of hickeys, his cock being stroked and his ass totally filled. "Marcus, yes...!"

"Yes, Cole," Marcus murmured back. "Come for me. Only for me."

Cole's body complied easily, come splashing along his belly and Marcus's hand, until he sagged forward again onto the mattress. Arms and legs spread, literally pinned, Marcus finished fucking him, coming hard...and crying out Cole's name.

LAW

"How the hell...?" Law muttered on the other end of the computer screen—he didn't want to leave the hospital, needed to be near Julian, but he hated not being able to see Cole. "How long did he spend studying us before Paolo caught sight of him in the woods?"

Styx was pacing, his face drawn. Paolo was sitting quietly,

twisting his fingers together, the anger apparent on his face. They were men who, while familiar with failure, were also never going to accept it.

"This is fucking terrifying," Law continued.

"What the fuck is he trying to do?" Styx's voice came out low and even, but Law knew he was anything but.

"It's a taunt. That's why he didn't bother to run when he had Cole. It was like, look what I can do right in front of you," Law continued, his hands fisted on his lap. "He must think we're all Cole's customers or something...that we dragged him back into the life."

Paolo's voice was fierce when he told them, "I never thought I'd say this, but I sure as hell hope Cole's the first one he tried this with—because Cole's definitely going to be his last."

32

"I WANT TO GO WITH YOU," COLE INSISTED WHEN MARCUS informed him that he was going to the hospital where Julian was. Marcus was muttering something about how that was a really fucking bad idea, how they shouldn't get Cole involved in something like this. "I'm already involved," Cole reminded him.

"Yes, I remember Law brought you. And that I stupidly agreed to let you be bait. Not happening again." But in the end, Marcus brought Cole along because it would be good for both Cole and for Julian, and because Marcus refused to leave Cole behind. Law was in the building too. They knew they had to cover Cole closely, ever since he'd realized that the man who was after him was from the prison and not a customer at all, but rather a cop at the prison where Cole had remained for a month.

So they were, in a way, starting from scratch, although none of them doubted that Seth had training, military or otherwise.

Marcus's fingers flew over the keys. Hacking into the hospital's security system was the easy part. Figuring out the cameras that this guy might not have noticed would prove far more difficult. And then Marcus sat back, looked over at Julian and asked, "When the social worker came in, did he look at your chart?"

Julian nodded distractedly because he was playing a video game on the hospital TV. Marcus's eyes went to the metal-covered chart. "Was he wearing gloves?"

"Um...maybe? Although, no, I don't think so. He held my hand, so I think I would've remembered." Julian cut him a look. "Why?"

"No big deal. There's a flu outbreak, so the staff is supposed to be extra careful."

Julian seemed satisfied with the answer, or else too into his video game to worry about it. It allowed Marcus to dust the chart in the bathroom and send the fingerprints on to Clint. Half an hour later, they came back with several hits—hospital personnel...and one very interesting hit. A person who didn't exist. And Law and Marcus both knew how to trace those kinds of people.

Meanwhile, Cole was sitting with Paolo, watching hours of videotape taken at the hospital, starting the morning that Julian said the social worker had been to see him. But nobody looked familiar or out of place or suspicious.

They were right outside the room, in the waiting area by the nurses' station, under the cameras themselves.

"What if we try the night before?" Cole asked.

"You mean, when you and Law went to first visit Julian?" Paolo rubbed his chin. "Yeah. Or maybe even the night before that. Maybe this guy kind of trolls the hospital, looking for guys like Julian." Cole paused. "That would be around the time he realized I wasn't waiting for him, playing his game. It's like he made the decision to actively look for somebody new at that point."

Paolo pressed some keys and brought up footage starting two days before Cole and Law met Julian for the first time in the hospital. Cole leaned on his elbows, his eyes blurry, but he forced himself to watch. He could only fast-forward so much, because he really had to concentrate on the faces, faces he wasn't even sure he'd remember. But he had to hope that something, someone, would jog his memory. They were too close for him to give up now.

It was close to four hours later when Paolo told Cole he needed to get some sleep before he could continue, but right then something—someone—caught Cole's eye. He leaned forward, and Paolo noticed immediately, paused the tape and rewound a little bit. Cole narrowed his eyes and watched the crowd of people herd into the emergency room. There'd been a fight in the corner and everybody went towards it, except for a lone man in a white coat who'd glanced over to the melee and then put his head down and continued through the doctors' entrance.

Paolo froze the tape on the man's face then punched a few keys and brought it to the forefront and into sharper focus. Cole stared and then his mouth opened.

"I think we've got a hit," Paolo murmured as Marcus came toward them.

"That's good, because we also have a name but no picture." Marcus leaned in to stare at the man. "That's Seth Rogers. Former Army and former CIA. He's so fucked up that the only way he got the cop gig was to falsify his old records. Definitely a psych case, even before the CIA took him on. But after that, forget it."

Cole just shook his head, wondering how he could've been

so wrong, how he could've forgotten about this guy. But his time spent with him had been seemingly nonexistent. It's not like he had regular conversations with the prison staff. It'd been such a painful time in Cole's life he'd basically been on autopilot the entire time, and those guards? Now barely a blip.

"Sometimes that's all it takes," Paolo told him gently after Cole admitted all of that.

"Law is taking over for Marcus so you two can go home, okay? After what happened, it's not good for you to be here."

"Yeah, I need that," Cole heard himself say before he could stop himself. "I mean—"

"It's not a bad thing," Marcus told him. And Cole really wanted to believe that.

33

MARCUS AND COLE TOOK A CRAZY, MAZELIKE WAY OUT OF THE hospital and finally ended up in Marcus's truck.

"Did you do something to the windows?" Cole asked.

"Tinted them," Marcus said, then stared at Cole before putting the truck into gear. "It's bulletproof."

"The glass?"

"The whole thing," Marcus confirmed.

"When did that happen?"

"Always was," Marcus admitted, and Cole leaned back and closed his eyes. Marcus really had been protecting him from the start...and himself too. Which made Cole remember how much Marcus had been through in his life. Most PIs didn't have trucks like this.

They drove in silence, and Cole didn't mind. Marcus was concentrating on not being followed, and Cole attempted to clear his mind, to figure out the next steps.

He'd told Law he wanted to help him at the center. Law hadn't said yes immediately, for reasons other than the fact that he was being stalked. He didn't want Cole to be triggered. But he hadn't said no, either, so Cole figured Law would eventually warm to the idea.

Marcus pulled the truck all the way up the driveway but left plenty of room between the garage and the truck so cars could fit past it.

Or maybe he wasn't going close to it because he'd felt Cole tense up. Either way, Marcus was on his ass as they walked around the car and to the back porch. He checked the alarm from outside the house, showing Cole the rooms, and then he glanced up and said, "Shit, I meant to take in those garbage cans."

"I'll help."

"No, stay here. Keep an eye on the house." Marcus handed him a gun and shooed him inside, and Cole was too tired to argue, but still semi-annoyed he wasn't allowed to walk to the street to pull in a garbage can.

Then he thought about the recent attack and locked the door behind him. God, he hated this shit, being locked away and still feeling scared.

This wasn't over. It wouldn't be while Seth was alive.

He glanced at the monitors and saw Marcus circling the garbage cans and then, obviously satisfied, he started dragging them toward the garage. Cole followed him until he couldn't see Marcus, and then he turned away to try to see Marcus through the window.

But then he heard something...it wasn't loud, wasn't even a bump, and hell, maybe he sensed it more than heard it, but he turned to look out the side door and noticed movement by the garage. And a can, abandoned on its side.

Shit. He drew the weapon Marcus gave him and slid out the door as quietly as he could. He walked around the corner and looked...and saw Seth and Marcus at a standoff, with Marcus holding his gun on Seth, and Seth doing the same to Marcus. They were both perpendicular to him and maybe ten feet apart.

Had Seth been here, watching them pull in? Had Marcus known? All of that was running through Cole's mind, and he should've been relieved.

For the next long moment, Cole couldn't tear his eyes from Seth's profile.

It happened in seconds and yet somehow all seemed to be in slow motion. The only thing in his mind was *Save Marcus*. But as shots rang from Seth's gun, Marcus dove forward at the same time a bullet passed through Seth's forehead.

One shot. That was all it took.

Cole's mouth dropped as Seth's face sagged, his eyes open, the gun clattering to the ground before his body crumpled and fell with a hard *whoosh* onto the pavement, his head slamming with a crack as loud as the bullet. Blood pooled, and Cole couldn't take his eyes from Seth, didn't pull his gun away...not until he was completely reassured the man couldn't get back up and hurt Marcus.

Marcus rolled, jumped to his feet and said, "Baby...I'm fine. Stay right where you are."

Cole might've nodded, but he couldn't be sure. He watched Seth intently, saw Marcus's fingers on Seth's neck for several seconds.

Then Marcus told him, "He's gone."

He's gone.

As Cole processed that, Marcus walked to him, taking the gun from him and dialing his phone. "Yes, I'd like to report a shooting." He gave the address then said, "We have one man down."

He hung up and shoved his phone back into his pocket and said gently, "Cole, please go back inside."

"Why?"

Marcus stared at him with a tight shake of his head. "I've got this."

He wasn't sure what happened next—not beyond having a semipanic attack, and then he was coming to with Marcus's arms around him.

"Jesus, I'm so sorry. Didn't mean to scare you like that...if I could've warned you..." Marcus was telling him.

"'S'okay. I get it."

Marcus put a hand on his forehead. "You're cooling down. Your pulse is back to normal."

"It's really over?"

"Yeah, really over."

Cole buried his face against Marcus's chest. "The police?"

"They're here. The EMTs too."

"Great. This is becoming a fucking habit."

"Not after this, baby." Marcus helped him walk toward the house. "The police want to talk to us. So just tell them what happened."

And when the police questioned Cole, none of them seemed out to get anyone—this was simply about protocol and paperwork, and being told he was very lucky.

In the aftermath, Cole sagged against the chair. The questioning had taken those last bits of adrenaline from him, and he barely processed the police officer telling him they'd contact him if they needed anything further.

He reached and grabbed for Law's wrist, managed, "Marcus?"

"He's almost done. Come on—let's go sit on the couch." Law helped him head to the living room, where he sat next to Law.

Styx came in and they waited for what seemed like forever, until the detectives and Paolo came out of the sunroom. Marcus followed seconds later, and Cole didn't ask what happened. He was simply grateful that Marcus was coming toward him, sitting next to him, murmuring.

He fell asleep against Marcus's shoulder after shaking his head when Marcus asked if he wanted to see a doctor. He might've said that he needed sleep—and Marcus—but when he opened his eyes, he was in the same position. Law was still at his left, and Cole was still snuggled against Marcus. Paolo and Styx were in the chairs along the wall, and the TV was on in the semidark room, the volume low.

The first thing he did was ask, "Is it really over?"

"It is. They're calling it self-defense and closing the case," Marcus said.

"Because it fucking was," Law growled, and Cole concurred with a nod. "Seth's records showed how unstable he really was. He hid that record in order to get into the Academy. He hid his psychosis."

"So it wasn't anything I did," Cole said quietly, more to himself than anyone else, but still they'd heard him.

"Jesus, Cole." Marcus looked horrified. "Not at all. Why would you think that?"

Cole turned to him. "Because of what you said to me. You told me that I did things to rich men. Maybe I got him mad or unwittingly made him think..."

"Stop." Marcus took him by the shoulders. "I was an asshole for accusing you the way I did. But even if you did do something to him—led him on in the name of the job—it doesn't give anyone the right to threaten your life. But fuck, I believe you—I trust you. Okay?"

He nodded, because nodding was easy. Believing what Marcus told him? That was another thing entirely.

But Marcus was shaking his head, telling him, "You did nothing. The guy was sick. Disturbed."

But Cole couldn't get the idea out of his head that one day he might say something completely innocuous and that would set somebody off again. Which was totally ridiculous, of course, because who lived their life like that?

Somebody who'd almost gotten killed by a stalker. "At least Julian doesn't have to know about this. Paolo was right—some things are better kept to yourself."

Marcus nodded, but he still looked worried. "You need to stop worrying—everyone's safe, especially you. You need rest."

But Cole shook his head. "Julian's going over to the shelter tonight. I'd like to be there to help him get settled in. Law said he'd take us."

Cole hadn't realized what he'd said, or how it sounded, until he saw the flash of hurt cross Marcus's face. To his credit, Marcus only nodded and smiled and said, "I know that's important to you. I'll be waiting here when you get back. From there we'll talk about what's next."

We'll talk about what's next. That echoed in Cole's brain for the rest of the night.

The worst was over, because Marcus considered *the worst* the fact that Cole had nearly been killed. But now that he was safe and Seth was dead, all the other obstacles Marcus had pushed to the back burner were layered up and threatened to catch fire.

Cole was talking about getting a new apartment, or at least moving back into his old one. Going back to his life the way it was before Seth. He'd actually said that out loud before their very late dinner tonight after getting Julian settled in the halfway house. He'd used the words "going back to my life" as if his time with Marcus was simply an unwanted intrusion and something that was never going to be a part of his life long term.

Marcus had told them he wasn't hungry, that he wanted to go for a run instead, and Cole either didn't notice Marcus was upset or pretended not to. And so Marcus had run a good six or seven or maybe even eight miles—he'd lost count along the way—and now he kicked around the backyard of his three bosses' house, trying to summon the courage to go inside, pack and go back to his own place. His own life.

"He didn't mean it like that, you know." Law sat on the small stone wall surrounding the outer edges of the property.

"You're working on being a ghost now?"

"It just comes naturally." Law handed him a bottle of water. "He thinks that maybe we only had him here as a job. He thinks he might only be a job to you. You're both thinking the same stupid shit, and you're tripping all over each other."

"I didn't realize that Phoenix, Inc. employed relationship counselors."

"It's not that the sarcasm isn't appreciated," Law started, "but I figured I'd save you the trouble of making the same stupid, pigheaded mistakes the three of us almost made."

"And suppose I tell him what I want, and he doesn't want that, doesn't want me? Suppose he just wants to go back to his old life. Suppose he really meant that?"

"You're not going to know unless you ask. Don't you need to put it to rest either way?"

"I've never liked you," Marcus muttered, and Law simply laughed.

34

WHEN MARCUS WENT UP TO THE ROOM HE'D BEEN SHARING WITH Cole, as he suspected, he found Cole packing.

Cole looked up when Marcus came in, a flash of guilt in his eyes. "Leaving?" Marcus asked, trying to keep his voice casual and not angry.

"Yeah. I mean, I wasn't going to go without saying anything. I wasn't sneaking out." Cole sighed. "I never expected any of this, Marcus. I don't know what the fuck to do."

Marcus sat on the bed next to him. "I didn't either. But I do know what I want to do."

Cole smiled. "Well yeah, we're good at that."

"That's not the only thing I'm talking about, Cole. Sex with you is great, but I'm not... I want to be with you. Go to sleep with you. Wake up with you. I want to give us a chance. I want you to move in with me."

Cole drew in a surprised breath. "Shit. Marcus, you've got to understand...I really want that."

"So do it."

"I can't." Cole stared at the floor for a second, then back up at Marcus, explaining, "It's just that everything happened so fast. I need to be sure that this isn't all about the job or the danger or guilt for you."

"Or for you," Marcus said quietly, and Cole didn't disagree. Okay then, so that was out on the table. Marcus supposed that was better than nothing. "I still want to see you. Date you. Be with you." Because he wanted to be as clear as possible on that.

Cole smiled shyly. "Yeah, I'd like that too."

Marcus sighed with relief. He'd forgotten in all of this just how much Cole had been through, even before the stalker. This had been a two-week-long frenzy, and at times it almost seemed like it'd been a dream. "Why don't you come to my place tonight—my apartment. You've never been there. I'd like to cook you dinner."

"That sounds great, but I think...can we wait until tomorrow night? I think I need a night to myself."

Even though Marcus didn't want to agree, he did. He was slightly relieved that Cole agreed to the dinner, but too much could happen until then to make Cole blow him off. He wouldn't let Cole beg off on dinner because that was only part one of Marcus's plan...the other part included the rental apartment in his place. And Cole firmly moved in there. At least until Marcus could convince him to move in with Marcus completely.

Cole stood in the doorway of his old apartment, flashing back to the bomb, to finding pictures...to how alone he'd been before Marcus and the others circled around him and saved him. But he didn't hesitate longer than a few seconds because Paolo had dropped him off and he would be concerned. So he turned and waved, and Paolo waved back and pulled his truck out of the driveway.

Cole stepped inside, closed and locked the door behind him as a safety precaution. He used the alarm that Marcus and Law had installed days earlier, and once it was armed, he felt marginally better. But he couldn't bring himself to unpack. It didn't feel like home anymore. Paolo's house was a home, although granted, not his home.

The problem was, Cole had begun to feel like his home was wherever Marcus was. And even though Marcus would've been cool with that right now, they didn't know each other. They knew facts. They knew each other's bodies. But how could something that happened so fast be any good? How could it last?

To stop himself from thinking, he went through his usual routine of shadowboxing and jump rope, blasting the music in his ears. And then he showered and got ready for a sleep that would never come.

He could've accepted Marcus's invite, even at this late hour. In his heart, he knew that it would be easy enough to even surprise him, to get on his bike and ride through the highways with the wind in his hair, the rumble of the bike clearing his head.

Deep, wrenching sobs tore from his throat. Because this wasn't where he wanted to be, and certainly not alone. He shoved his fist against his mouth, mainly because he didn't want to hear himself cry. Made him angrier and sadder than he already was. Made him feel weak.

Made him *feel*...and, like Marcus, up until this point Cole'd been good at keeping it all turned off.

Get it together. Because he'd been the one to make the clean break. Figured it would be easier on everyone—except himself —but that didn't matter. It never really had.

A sudden knock at the door made him start. He stood, glanced out the window and saw Marcus's truck. Before he could remind himself he looked like he'd been crying, he flung the door open to find Marcus leaning against the doorjamb, looking too damned good in a pair of worn jeans and a simple black T-shirt.

And he was holding a bakery box. "It's apple. Your favorite," he told Cole. But he pushed in and put the box down, and before Cole could say anything, he brushed a thumb at the tears in the corners of Cole's eyes. He studied them, then wisely didn't mention anything about that, instead saying, "I wanted to make sure you were coming to dinner."

"You don't have to cook for me anymore."

"I never had to do that for you. I wanted to. I still want to," Marcus told him, his voice steady and calm, like he was determined not to start a fight, no matter how hard Cole might push him.

"Okay, fine."

"I'd like you to stay over too. At least think about it."

"Marcus—"

"It's what people who are dating do. We blew through any normal stage of dating we might've had. And there's nothing wrong with that but still..." Marcus's thumb moved down to trace Cole's jawline, "...I like having you with me."

God, he sounded so sincere. He really did. And so Cole shoved one of his still-packed bags on his shoulder.

"You could take all of it," Marcus said.

"Fuck. Marcus..."

"I've got an apartment in my house. I've been looking to rent it."

"And you're just telling me this now because?"

"I thought it would piss you off if I mentioned it earlier."

"It would've." Marcus knew him well, it seemed. He'd let Cole come home alone because he must've known it would be tough.

But maybe it'd been hard for Marcus to go home alone as well, and that was something Cole hadn't taken into consideration. Maybe this wasn't as one-sided as he'd feared.

Marcus was waiting for his answer, but he pushed, just a little. "I want you close. I want you with me...in my bed, among other things. But if you need to be independent, I get it. Still, being independent and being alone are two different things."

Cole stuffed his hands into his jeans pockets. "I don't know how to do this."

"Do whatever feels right. Does this feel right?" Marcus asked as he moved closer, rubbed the back of Cole's neck the way Cole had comforted him. Then his hand moved to Cole's shoulder, a caress that made him shiver. "Or does this?"

Cole didn't have to say anything. He melted against Marcus, let Marcus pull him in for a kiss. It was so full of reassurances.

"I'm hungry," he murmured, his lips still inches from Marcus's, and his stomach growled in agreement. "And I'm paying you rent."

"I'm not going to argue with whatever keeps you close," Marcus told him. "Let's get your bags."

Cole rode his bike behind Marcus's truck because he needed to. And when he pulled into the garage next to him, Marcus smiled and hugged him, and any last bit of Cole's nerves instantly faded. It felt the same. It was the same.

And he went inside and they sat at the table and they ate

dinner that Marcus had made just for him, plus the pie, and they laughed and they joked. They attempted to watch a movie, but then Marcus's hands started to wander. Cole let them.

They ended up in Marcus's bed.

"Stay. Stay the night in my bed, at least." Marcus's arms were wrapped around Cole, as if not wanting to give him the choice. And Cole was actually okay with that.

"I'll stay here."

"Good. One more thing. I have an event to go to in a couple of days. It's a black-tie event, which I realize doesn't sound like all that much fun. But the food will be good." Marcus smiled. "I'm really selling it, aren't I?"

Cole laughed. "You had me at food. But I don't have a tux."

"Everybody needs a tux, so we'll go get you one. My treat, okay?"

"Marcus, I can't—"

"I insist. You wouldn't need it if I didn't invite you. It's only fair."

Cole conceded, because honestly, if he was gonna spend money on something, it wouldn't be a monkey suit.

"And...while I've got you really agreeable..." Marcus said.

"Marcus..." Cole warned him. "I'm not a fucking pushover."

"No you're not. But you're turning me into one," Marcus growled. "Come on. I need you to approve your apartment, and then that will be settled and I can drag you back to my bed. Where you belong."

Cole let Marcus pull him out of bed and together, naked, they walked downstairs, turned down a hallway until they came to a locked door, where Marcus handed him the key. "Rent's due on the first of the month."

"You had this all planned."

"Totally. You can't blame me for not wanting you in your old place. I don't think you're entirely comfortable there anymore. And so you'll spend nights here with me because you don't want to be alone there. And that's not going to help you know whether or not you're with me because of me…or because you need an escape." Marcus paused. "No strings, Cole. If things go bad between us…I want you in my life. Okay?"

Cole used the key and opened the apartment door. "I can't fucking afford this."

"Yeah, you can."

He wanted to argue with Marcus, but, fuck, everything in his gut told him this was right. "Fine. But you're accepting my money."

"I know that."

At least Cole's boss had agreed to give him his old job back. He'd start tomorrow. "Fine. It's a deal."

"Good. Back to bed. You'll be agreeing to more things before I'm through," Marcus promised.

The next night, after work, Cole turned in his notice to his old landlord, who was pretty understanding, and then he rode his Harley over to Marcus's. When he opened the door and took his bags from where Marcus had left them, right near the stairs leading to Marcus's own bedroom, of course, he dumped his bags inside the apartment space as he heard Marcus coming down the stairs.

But really, seeing this place in the fading daylight made him realize how much Marcus really did care about him.

"Hey, things okay?" Marcus sounded concerned, probably because Cole was just standing there staring.

Okay? It was gorgeous. A large, loftlike space that was furnished, freshly painted, with dark hardwood floors that were pristine. It was better than he'd remembered it from last night. He cleared his throat before saying, "Yeah, it's pretty perfect."

"Be more perfect if you were staying with me." Cole turned to him. "Marcus..."

"I know, I know. But don't expect not to share a bed with me, Cole. I've gotten too used to that."

Cole had too. And so he let Marcus pull him into his arms. In turn, Cole wrapped his arms around Marcus's shoulders and stared up at him. "It's really over with Seth, right?"

"He's gone, Cole. He's never going to hurt you again," Marcus said gently.

Marcus had killed for him. His life—all of their lives—had been in danger...and instead of Cole having to live every day wondering if Seth was going to escape prison or defy his restraining order, Marcus had taken care of it.

After they'd gotten Cole's things inside, it was time for a run to the tailor, who'd agreed to have Marcus and Cole come in after closing time.

Marcus told Cole he'd help him unpack later, although really, he planned on making sure Cole put that off for as long as possible. To that end, he'd put on a delicious-smelling stew that he knew would immediately distract Cole when they walked back into the house. Now, inside the expensive, exclusive men's shop, Marcus watched Cole trying on various tuxes and coming out to look at himself in the big mirrors. He listened to the tailor, smiled when he noticed Marcus staring at him. But, in general, Cole seemed genuinely unfazed by the wealth. It wasn't that he didn't notice it, because he did and he surveyed it coolly as if he recognized it as a long-lost enemy, but it didn't affect him. It didn't make him shrink back or slump his shoulders or do anything differently. He was still simply Cole, with his rumpled hair and his well-fucked looks.

Except these days, Marcus was the one putting those looks on his face.

Now, Cole sat next to him as they waited for the tailor to do a few quick alterations before calling it a night.

"How was work?" Marcus asked him.

"It's good to be back. Have a couple of classics to work on. But you know...I was thinking that there's something else I want to do."

"Volunteer with Law?"

"Well, yeah, that's a given. But I want to open a gym—a boxing gym. One where I can donate a lot of time to the kids at the shelter." He looked down at his new shoes and said, "I've been saving up. It's not enough, I know, but maybe I could get a loan."

And it was the sweetest goddamn thing he'd ever heard, and he knew deep in his heart that Cole wasn't asking him for the money or insinuating that at all...but still every single fucking ridiculous alarm bell in Marcus's head went off. "That sounds like a great idea," he said noncommittally.

Cole cocked his head and looked at him funny. He just nodded like he'd expected a different kind of answer, or maybe a little more enthusiasm, but he just shrugged. And then the tailor called him over to try on the tux again.

You are so fucked up, Marcus.

"You are so fucked up, Marcus," Clint told him an hour later, when Cole had gone to his apartment to unpack, something Marcus had desperately not wanted him to do earlier.

And now? He was really thrown. And fucked up.

Completely. "What's wrong with me, Clint? And please be more specific," he said now.

He'd sought his old friend out and now he sat at his kitchen table, Skyping with Clint, and he couldn't disagree with what Clint was saying. But that didn't help anything.

"So let me get this straight." Clint pointed at him. "Cole mentions wanting to open a boxing gym to help the shelter kids. Kids who were just like he was."

"Not like he wants to buy clothes or a new car or a big house. He wants to open a gym to help shelter kids, and you've somehow interpreted that as he wants to use you for your money." And that last part was told to Marcus by Jace, Clint's boyfriend, who Marcus hadn't asked to get involved but, hell, when it was laid out like that...

"I've been used before" was all he said.

"Does Cole even know you have money?" Jace asked.

Marcus looked at Clint. "I didn't realize he was a part of this conversation."

"Good luck trying to stop him. Besides that, he's doing a damn good job of showing you what an ass you're being," Clint said, and Jace simply smiled.

"Okay, no, he doesn't know how much money I have. I mean, he knows I've got money but...I don't think he's got a real grasp of it."

"Did he ask you to cosign a loan?" Jace continued.

"No," he ground out.

Jace threw his hands in the air as if Marcus was hopeless and walked out of the room, muttering to himself.

"You've started thinking about the fucking black-ops job again," Clint said, wagging his finger at Marcus through the screen. "It's like your form of fucking penance. And it's running. Stay with Cole and figure your shit out."

Marcus hated how right Clint was—and Jace too—and how wrong he was...and how much his past dogged him. "I will," he said finally, and he meant it. To show Clint how serious he was, he held up his phone after blocking the guy's number who called him about the jobs.

"It's a first step," Clint told him. "Now keep moving forward."

35

IT WAS GETTING HARDER TO IGNORE THE FACT THAT MARCUS HAD some real money. Cole didn't know if Marcus was self-made or if it was family money, but between the beach house, the main house with the apartment and tux shopping...well, the writing was on the wall.

And since Cole knew that the money thing was one of Marcus's hang-ups, he wasn't quite sure how to deal with it. He was definitely able to go with the flow of things...to a point. But when he was walking into things completely unprepared, his defenses immediately went up.

As they were now, as Marcus drove them to the event. Which, it turned out, according to the invitation, was some kind of gala. Which made it seem far grander than an event. And Marcus was barely talking now, just staring straight ahead, which made Cole even more uncomfortable.

Things hadn't been right since the fitting the night before. They'd had sex—and they were good at sex, but right after-ward, even though Marcus threw his arm across Cole and fell asleep, things had been off.

Maybe it's because we were both almost killed by a stalker. In a way, that was still hovering over them. Cole had woken up in a cold sweat about it last night, but Marcus hadn't...and Cole hadn't wanted to burden him.

God, you really suck at this relationship shit.

"We'll be there in ten," Marcus told him now.

"Okay, great." Cole shifted. "So, this money thing..." he started, and Marcus shrugged. "Family money. I inherited some, but I'm also good with investments. It's the family business. Just because I chose another route for my career didn't mean I didn't inherit the gift for it. Is that a problem for you?"

"Not for me. But I know you're touchy about it."

"Touchy, yeah," Marcus echoed.

Hell, this was not the kind of conversation they should be having right before some kind of fancy gala thing. This was the kind of thing that made Cole realize that maybe they didn't know each other at all, that maybe the past month had been built on sex and danger alone.

And he let those thoughts freak him the fuck out, enough so that he hadn't noticed Marcus had pulled over right outside the gates of a massive-looking mansion with grand grounds and luxury cars and limos pulling into the long driveway.

Oh fuck me. "Is this what you didn't want to tell me?" Cole asked, unable to stop his eyes from widening in surprise and slight horror at the venue. "Because your family's name's on the side of the goddamned building."

Marcus gripped the wheel tightly and nodded. "Like I said, my family's got some money."

Cole's neck snapped toward him. "Ya think? And you didn't think it was important to tell me until right this minute?"

"Cole—"

"There's still no trust there."

"Look, in my experience, people always want something, whether it's money, reputation or power. Most people who want that don't deserve it. I didn't earn my family's money, which was why I went out and worked for a living. I put my inherited money in trust and gave a lot of it to charities. So I don't have money to hand out. I don't bankroll projects, okay?"

"What the fuck—did you memorize that speech? Do you give it on second dates?" Cole asked. "And what projects are you talking about?"

Marcus turned to him. "I just want to make it clear...the gym you were talking about..."

"You're fucking kidding me, aren't you?" Cole demanded. "I didn't ask you for shit. I didn't even think...fuck, but you did. That's the first thing you thought of. The first thing you're always going to think of whenever I mention anything like that. Christ, we can survive almost being killed together but your money issues will tear us apart."

"Money makes people do weird things, Cole," Marcus told him, an edge to his voice. "Everyone always has something to gain."

"Like you didn't gain anything from your family's money?" Cole challenged. "You know what I gained from my family? Pretty much life, and that's it, Marcus, so the next time you're going to accuse me of shit, get your facts straight. Because I turned down money. A hell of a lot of it too. You think guys didn't want to buy me full time? I had plenty of sugar daddies lined up—all I had to do was say the word."

"But you didn't."

"Never."

Marcus sat stiffly. "This was a bad idea."

"Yeah, I'm guessing so."

"Not bringing you, Cole. Nothing about you."

Cole definitely didn't believe him. "You should've told me about this ahead of time. You can't throw this shit on me."

And then he opened the door and got out, all the while wanting to hear Marcus call for him, wanting Marcus to stop him...

All the while knowing that wouldn't happen. And when he got the courage to finally turn, he saw that Marcus's car was gone from the curb, no doubt swallowed up in the line for the gala.

He stuffed his hands into his pants pockets and kept going in the opposite direction.

As he walked along, he thought about Law. What Law would do in this case. But he realized that the only thing that mattered is what he himself wanted to do. What he was going to do. And he realized that he didn't have to wonder. Instead of guessing, he pulled out his phone, and he dialed.

"You've already made up your mind" was one of the first things Law said after Cole told him the story.

Marcus had only watched Cole's back in the rearview mirror for a few long moments before he'd pulled away and into the valet line for the party.

He didn't want to be back here, mentally or physically. Dammit. He thought Cole could heal him—and fuck it all, he had. Marcus guessed he hadn't done the same for Cole.

Yeah, I'm totally fucked up. And I just let the best thing that ever happened to me walk away.

But he steeled himself, and he went inside and he began the serious business of bullshitting and air kissing. Shaking hands, pasting on a smile and pretending all was right with the world.

"Marcus, I was hoping you'd be here." Claude, his ex, was

standing in front of him, holding two glasses of champagne, one of which he handed to Marcus.

"Thanks." Marcus accepted the glass and took a small sip, then a larger one. He'd take a cab home if he had to.

"You look great."

"You too." Marcus had long ago grown indifferent to the man who'd once sliced out his heart. Claude dated many of the wealthy men in his community, although he got away with it because of his good looks and his ability to reflect well on whomever he was dating. Really, it had been Marcus's fault—he'd assumed far too much for a first-time love. But that didn't mean that the ache inside of him wasn't cavern-sized now, thanks to Cole.

"You're not seeing anyone?" Claude asked.

Marcus opened his mouth, then realized he had no fucking idea what to say, because any of it would make him sound pathetic.

It was then that Cole slid a hand through his arm and across his lower back. "Sorry I'm late—what did I miss?"

Marcus stared at him. Blinked. Cole gave him a small smile—part fierce pride, part apology for his role in the fight...and hell, Cole had nothing to apologize for. Marcus's hand went up to give an unmistakably intimate rub to the back of Cole's neck. "Need a drink?"

Cole looked at the one in Marcus's hand and said "I'll be driving later" so suggestively that Claude choked on his own drink.

Until then, Marcus had forgotten Claude. Now his ex was standing there gaping at them. "Oh sorry—Cole, this is Claude."

"Hey." Cole stuck out a hand and Marcus watched, bemused. "Gonna steal him away."

Cole coughed and Marcus sighed internally, and right then and there, he knew it was all over for him...and that he'd never really stood a chance against Cole.

Cole was smaller, but he could fight. He was tough. That alone made Marcus's cock hard. Marcus had always known how protective he was, but hell, Cole was actually a little... growly. And as handsome as he was, an angry Cole was a little goddamned scary.

And hot. And he told Cole that.

"Shut up, Marcus." Cole shoved him playfully. "Do you need me to take you to the bathroom to shut you up?"

"Probably, yes."

Cole nodded—no smile breaking through. But Marcus's hard cock was telling him everything he needed to know. "Want me to kick Claude's ass?"

"I told you I don't care about him. I only care about you."

Cole's expression softened a bit. "I still want to kick his ass though."

"I don't blame you." And when Marcus walked Cole away from the main crowd into a more private space, he said, "You're fucking moving in with me. Fuck the other apartment, okay? You're moving in with me and you're marrying me. That's it, I'm done."

Cole's eyes widened. "You're so motherfucking romantic."

"I'll try to keep it toned down."

Cole swallowed noticeably hard. "I love you, Marcus. Better than that, I trust you."

"That's a yes then?"

"Definitely."

Marcus smiled. "I suppose it's time for you to meet the family you're marrying into."

.   .   .

"Are you sure about this?" Cole asked. He had no doubts about being with Marcus— not anymore, but meeting the family...

"Very. Come on."

But as he walked in next to Marcus and eyes turned in his direction, he knew that it wasn't going to go well. He'd worked parties like this, so he knew the deal.

Marcus's family greeted him with what could only be called light disdain. At best. "Cole, lovely to meet you." Marcus's mom's voice dripped with a haughty accent that told everyone she believed exactly the opposite of what she said. "How did you meet Marcus?"

"At work."

"You're a PI, then?"

"No, an auto mechanic. I work on Harleys too."

"Really. So you don't have much in common with him then?"

He was about to say "not beyond cock" when Marcus stepped in. "Mother, really?"

"It's a fact, Marcus." She fluffed the back of her hair with a perfectly manicured hand.

"If that was the only issue, I could ignore it. But he's a baby."

"*He's* standing right here, sweetheart." Cole smiled innocently.

"Come on, let's mingle." Marcus tugged his arm while Cole was mentally patting himself on the back for rendering Marcus's mother speechless.

He was sure it wouldn't last long though. "I want to get out of here."

"I understand. I really do. But I'm here for a specific purpose. Trust me, this isn't my regular scene," Marcus assured him.

Just then, there was an announcement booming through

the room that asked for Marcus, the head of the Give Back charity, to please come to the podium.

Marcus glanced at Cole as he reached into his jacket pocket and pulled out what Cole assumed was a speech.

"This is your charity?"

Marcus nodded. "I started it about five years ago, by proxy. I wanted to accomplish what I wanted to, the way I wanted to, so I figured this could become my karma."

"Did it?"

He stared at Cole for a long moment before stroking the back of his neck. "I'm looking right at him."

"Jesus, Marcus." He grabbed the man's forearm and held on.

"We can leave after I give my speech."

"I'm okay with staying. I'm better now."

"Yeah, better than anyone here, Cole. I need you to believe that."

"With you next to me, I finally do."

36

LAW

It wasn't until Law got a text from Cole, telling him that Marcus was giving a speech and that things were okay, that he went upstairs to the two men waiting for him.

Styx and Paolo were also okay, and they'd started without him. Law took a moment in the doorway to watch the scene unfolding. Paolo was naked, wrapped around Styx, who was also naked. Styx's cock slid in between Paolo's ass cheeks, teasing him, while Styx sucked on his nipple.

That drove Paolo nuts. Law smiled at the keening cries coming from Paolo—he could be really demanding when he wanted something. And since he'd known this day was coming, he'd been angling to make it happen sooner, or using it as fodder for teasing every time they had sex.

Because, hell yeah, just thinking about what they'd done with him last year was enough to make Law impossibly hard. He stripped as he walked across the room toward the bed, bent down to lick Styx's cock and tease Paolo's ass while Styx forced Paolo up and down.

"Jesus," Paolo groaned. "You two...going to fucking kill me."

"Not a bad way to go," Styx murmured. "Yeah, Law, right there."

Law planned on torturing both men tonight, and he licked and laved and made sure they were both so close to coming themselves that it hurt to hold back. They were cursing him by the time he'd finished, and Styx threatened him that he was going to find himself in Paolo's position if he wasn't careful.

With that, Paolo glanced over his shoulder. "I think he's trying not to be careful."

"You're not getting out of this," Law told him. "It's tradition."

"Doesn't mean we couldn't start a new one," Styx mused. "Whoever's the most deserving."

"The one who drove us the most crazy in the past year," Paolo added. "It definitely wasn't me this time."

Law shook his head slowly, pressing his chest to Paolo's back, his cock rubbing along Styx's. "None of what happened this past month was my fault."

"It's not about fault, Law. Never is, never was," Styx told him, his voice rough, and oh fuck, they were both seriously considering switching this around.

That's not to say he hadn't thought about it himself once or twice, hadn't wondered what it would be like with Styx and Paolo.

"Has he done it before?" Paolo asked Styx.

"He's right in the room," Law reminded him with a hard nip on his shoulder.

"Just once." Styx's eyes burned into his. "It'd be much better with us."

"That I agree with," Law said. "But we're not changing this now. Because Paolo wants this."

Paolo didn't argue, not when Law held his hips still, picked him up slightly so Styx wasn't in the way and began to press inside him. Paolo scrambled to hold on to Styx's shoulders as Law pushed into Paolo's already well-lubed ass, a tight, hot hug around his cock that would get hotter and tighter once Styx joined him.

"Need to get you ready, baby."

Styx moved back to sit against the headboard and Paolo got onto his hands and knees for a few minutes, taking Styx's cock in his mouth as Law rode him. Styx's hand wound in Paolo's hair, and his eyes met Law's. They were joined in ways Law had never thought possible—and ways he was so glad he hadn't missed out on. It would've been so easy for one of them to walk away in the beginning, when Styx first reentered his life and things with Paolo were so new and fragile.

But they'd persevered. They'd become a force to be reckoned with, in so many ways.

"You ready?" Styx asked him.

Paolo nodded, almost like he couldn't trust his voice. Law could understand that—this was a lot to deal with physically, but it was an emotional mind blower on top of that. For all of them, but for Paolo...

He slid out of Paolo and let the man straddle Styx, taking him deep inside. Styx pumped his hips up into him for a few minutes while Law enjoyed watching them, running his tongue down Paolo's back, making him shudder and groan.

Finally, Law moved chest to back with Paolo again. Styx was propped up on pillows so he could easily enjoy the show, but he stilled the way Paolo did when Law began the slow, smooth process of joining Styx's cock inside Paolo.

Paolo was holding Styx's chest, his hands white, and Styx would bear bruises. He also wouldn't care—none of them would.

By this time, Law and Styx had already opened Paolo up with their fingers and cocks, and now he was riding Styx. Law took advantage of that, slapping Paolo's ass. For some reason, it made Paolo shudder, a whole-body shudder that both men noticed immediately.

Suddenly, it was almost too much. He wanted to shake his head, tell them no, climb off Styx—and they'd let him, of course. But part of it was the escape, the chase. In this safe environment, he could do that, and these men he loved? They understood.

"Come on, baby. You know you want it." From anyone else but Styx, it would've sounded awful, sleazy even. From Styx, it was a simple statement, telling Paolo to not be ashamed of what he wanted.

Law took a different tactic, murmuring in his ear, "Should've taped it last time so he could watch himself." Styx nodded approvingly. "Maybe we shouldn't make that mistake again."

Jesus, they were going to tape this? Paolo sat up like he was ready to bolt, but Law's hands came down on his shoulders—steady, warm and reassuring. But also commanding.

He wasn't going anywhere.

Styx throbbed inside him. "You can't deny you've been thinking about it...wondering when it was going to happen again."

Paolo could deny it, of course, but he'd be lying. And since they'd mentioned it to him earlier this week, every time he saw the men his stomach tightened with anticipation. And they knew it, dammit, which was why they did it.

"And now we're safe," Law murmured, reading his mind.

Right. They were safe. Cole was safe, together with Marcus. Things were good.

Right here, in between the men he loved, things were fucking stupendous. "Now, Law," he ordered, and instead of a smart-ass answer or a joke, Law complied, pushing in with a hard thrust.

And that—that first push was always the hardest. His vision swam, his body tensed, although he knew he had to relax. Both Law and Styx were talking to him, rubbing him, relaxing him. And then Law was seated fully inside of him, next to Styx.

That's when the fireworks happened. None of them would last long—it didn't matter. The way he was angled, his gland got the benefit of all that constant driving pressure. Law was gripping him tight, cursing as he thrust, and Styx was trapped, watching Paolo carefully.

Law kissed the side of his neck, nipped him a little. Paolo jolted from that contact, and then Styx drove up hard.

"Fuck. Gonna come," Paolo panted.

"Not yet," Styx said, wrapping his fingers around the base of Paolo's cock to ensure that wouldn't happen.

Paolo's body was covered with a thin sheen of sweat, and he didn't know what the fuck to do with himself. He was complete sensation—didn't know how to handle it, to process it all. He needed relief, needed them to stop and to go, all at once.

He'd never get this from anyone else. They got him, and it made him want to laugh and cry at once. "Fucking love you," he managed, met Styx's eyes as Law nipped his earlobe.

"Love you, baby. Love you both," Styx said.

Law thrust again. Twice, hard. "Go, Paolo—don't hold back for us."

He didn't—he couldn't. He came with a burst of white-hot light as his climax hit him with a stunning force. His orgasm was protracted, like he'd been milked and couldn't stop it from happening.

He couldn't. Didn't want to. So he rode those waves, vaguely aware of Law, then Styx, losing it inside of him, which set off a fresh wave of contractions, pushing him to the brink.

He was leaning on Styx, unable to lie down until Law pulled out, which he did, slow and gentle. Styx remained inside him for a while, so he wouldn't be so empty, and he lay on Styx's chest, Law by their side, rubbing his back.

"Love," he murmured again, because that was all he had left. The best part was, it was all any of them had ever needed.

NEWSLETTER

Sign up for the newsletter of SE Jakes and her alter-ego Stephanie Tyler!

Be among the first to learn not only about new and upcoming books but also appearances and signings as well as special promotions and giveaways!

http://stephanietyler.com/newsletter/

INKED: HOLD THE LINE

INKED #1

**Catch up on HOLD THE LINE:
Book 1 in the Inked Series, on sale now!**

Holding on loosely has never been such a challenge...

What happens when a tattoo artist and a Delta Force soldier keep a promise and take a cross-country trip together? Quinn and Con are about to finally meet and find out.

Quinn thinks he's the responsible one, but he quickly learns that he needs to loosen up if he's got any shot of holding onto Con.

(This novella is now available as a standalone, but was previously published in the Danger Zone *Anthology, with all proceeds going to* Hope For the Warrior.*)*

Read Chapter One from *Hold The Line:*

Quinn McKenna glanced down at the stack of paper that had arrived certified mail just hours before, care of his younger brother, and then back up at the man hanging out by the pool table.

He didn't have a picture of Conlan "Con" Jenkins in his packet—just a basic description—but he realized now he'd have known the tall, handsome Delta Force soldier anywhere. There was something in his bearing that Quinn picked out easily. Maybe it was because Quinn's father and brothers had been Delta too, so he was in tune with the way they operated. Most of the Special Forces soldiers he'd come in contact with in his younger days, including his father and his brothers, appeared so outwardly casual to the rest of the world, blending in when they needed to. But Quinn knew that Con was consistently on alert, and that, if asked, he'd be able to give a description of every single person in the place tonight.

Bet you'll find him playing pool, Scott had also offered next to the name of the bar/restaurant picked for the initial meet-up, then added, *He'll be the one winning, with a lot of pissed-off guys around him.*

So yes, Quinn'd picked Con almost from the start, but remained at his table, casually scoping the soldier out while he ate dinner. He noted both he and Con were early for their meet-up, and wondered if they'd both been trying to outmaneuver the other. Not that there was any reason for that kind of thing—this was supposed to be a fun trip, not a competition. A trip ordered by Scott, and something neither Quinn nor Con could—or would—refuse.

Quinn could hear that phone conversation echoing in his ears.

"Bring my best friend to me," Scott had ordered him three

weeks ago on the phone, and in Con's paperwork, Quinn now saw that Scott had written, *Bring my brother home to me.*

When they'd spoken on the phone weeks earlier, Scott had also explained, "Con's dangerous with too much time on his hands."

Quinn remembered wanting to bang his head against the wall but had asked instead, "How dangerous?"

"You'll travel with him for a couple of weeks—you tell me."

Quinn immediately understood just what his brother meant, because Con was obviously well versed at hustling pool. The guys he'd been playing had gone from friendly to very disgruntled, and Con either noticed and didn't give a shit or else he was oblivious.

Quinn was betting on the former.

Then again, Con had refused the bets at least six times, had told the men asking that it wouldn't be fair, and not in a cocky, assholeish way. But the men weren't listening and Quinn knew there was a fight in Con's future. And that meant there'd be a fight in Quinn's as well.

There was still time to bail. He glanced at his watch, noting he was still early enough that Con wouldn't miss him if he left. Unless Con had pegged him from the moment he'd walked in.

Scott wants this, he reminded himself. And he wouldn't refuse his brother, no matter how badly he wanted to.

And he really wanted to. But Scott couldn't make this trip this year, not like he'd planned, and so he'd asked Quinn and Con to do it in his stead. They'd start here, outside of L.A. and end up in the Catskills, and ultimately, Scott's wedding, by way of the strange and varied path Scott had created for them.

By rights, Scott should've been here, a buffer between them, the glue that would bond them. Con and Scott had served together.

Sat on the bus together to Basic, and from that point forward they'd been inseparable. Con did come home with Scott for some holidays, but Quinn hadn't been there for any of those. He was the older brother, off sowing his wild oats, which was true. But during that time, he'd also become a licensed tattoo artist. He'd also been featured on a few of those ink shows on reality TV, but he had no real aspirations to be a regular, even though his boss wanted him to be. Mainly because the producers also wanted to include more about his personal life, thinking that would make for great TV.

But this wasn't TV—this was his motherfucking life, as he'd pointed out. His private life was private for a reason, although he'd never made any bones about his sexual orientation, or his bent toward BDSM. The writers of the show offered to find him love, especially if they could follow him into the club scene.

His boss at the tattoo shop told him he'd cave sooner than later. Right before he'd given Quinn the time off to make this road trip. And if that was a bribe, it was a pretty effective one. So he'd pushed back appointments. But really, Scott did the rest of the work, from the big things like booking hotels and restaurants to the mundane of actually planning the route (*"Con will tend to ramble and he doesn't like to use maps—says he doesn't need them"*)—and yeah, that was so *not* how Quinn operated.

But hell, he couldn't deny how handsome Con was. Not pretty boy, no. He was rugged looking, lanky with a swagger that probably made most guys want to be him or fall to their knees and beg to be fucked by him.

It made Quinn want to push Con to his knees and force his cock in between those full lips, watch them swell from sucking as his eyes glazed with pleasure.

You're supposed to be keeping an eye on him, not fucking him.

Did Scott even know if Con was gay, or bi? Did it matter?

What mattered was that this would be the longest trip of Quinn's life.

As soon as Con saw the pool table, he'd known he was fucked. Because he was nervous. Jumpy. And as much as playing pool always got him in shitloads of trouble, it also calmed him.

He'd come back to California forty-eight hours earlier after eight months OUTCONUS. He'd routed through his home post for seventy-two hours and then he'd literally come straight to this bar in Normalsville, USA.

He wasn't ready in any way, shape or form to be around civilians. Scott knew that—it was probably why he'd given Con a chaperone, in the form of Quinn McKenna.

Quinn'd arrived ten minutes after Con. Situational awareness was his job, and a guy like Quinn caught his attention easily. He'd seen pictures, but none had done Quinn justice. He'd walked in like he owned the place.

And he's bossy as fuck, Scott had told him often. And the way Quinn'd marched in, like he was planning on taking and conquering, made Con smile. Mainly because he didn't play by bossy rules. But looking at Quinn...maybe he should start.

Still, Con had been ignoring him for the better part of an hour, in favor of racking up. The pool cue, the chalk, the sharp snick of the balls as they snapped smartly together all drew him in, especially because of the way they mixed with the smell of beer and tobacco and cologne, all the bar chatter and music. The familiar sounds of his childhood.

And the people...he could group them easily, had been born and bred to group them in the most advantageous way possible. The monied set. The good ole boys. The cowards. The troublemakers.

Where Quinn fit in, Con had some idea, but he was open to really finding out. After a few games. And so he'd shot several, fucking up the first break the way he always did. His dad thought that Con had just perfected the art of the scam easily. Con had let him think it.

What was the alternative? *No, Dad. I really didn't fuck up my games on purpose—I let my nerves get the best of me...*

"You had a clear shot. Blind man could've made it."

Con didn't bother glancing up at the sound of the voice. Guaranteed, it was a plaid-shirted guy who'd been sitting at four o'clock, trying to pin him down for a so-called friendly game of pool.

Right now, Con screamed "easy betting money." But Con didn't want to bet on pool, hadn't planned on hustling tonight. The pressure had started from Plaid Shirt and then a few of his friends, and Con suggested they keep it friendly, play for beers. But the guys thought he was chicken. Goaded him.

Finally, because he needed to play pool and make them shut the fuck up, he took the bet. He figured he'd given them enough of an out that he didn't have to feel guilty. Now, an hour later, he was up two grand and up against three pissed-off regulars who would no doubt try to roll him in the parking lot when he left. At this point, they were in the "refusing to let him leave" stage of bargaining. The "just one more game" bullshit, like they'd suddenly get lucky.

Ain't happenin', boys.

Finally, Quinn'd sidled up to the table, looking like just another guy checking out the action. But he wasn't just another guy—he was big and tall and handsome...and he turned a lot of heads. He could probably fight well. But really, Con wouldn't have any problem taking on these guys the way he took their money. He'd told them not to—he'd been truthful, so that absolved him of any guilt he might've had.

Hell, he had enough guilt already—needed a fucking U-Haul for it—and wasn't looking to add more weight to pull.

Instead, he took a drink of the seltzer water that'd been fueling him most of the night and finally made eye contact with Quinn. The two of them were standing slightly away from the pool table, watching Plaid Shirt rack up—again—with the others watching him like they were afraid he'd just disappear into thin air.

Con could definitely do that, but it was more smoke and mirrors than anything. All of this was. So he stared at the big man who looked at him, disapproval written all over his face. It was literally going to be like being watched by Big Brother. Although he looked nothing like Scott, Scott had shared family pictures ad nauseam.

Con had none. In return for warm fuzzy family pictures and their accompanying stories (that Con had actually liked but would never come right out and admit to), Con taught Scott to hustle pool. Well, to assist. Hustling was a skill best learned young and used regularly, especially when someone was depending on it for survival. He'd learned early on that if he didn't hustle, he didn't eat. That's how he'd grown up.

"You're good," Quinn said in a low, deep voice.

"I know," he said irritably as Quinn's dark eyes locked him in place. He swallowed, forced himself to look away.

"How long are you going to keep this up?"

"I've been trying to get out of here for an hour."

"So go."

"Gotta give them a chance to make their money back. Wouldn't be fair otherwise," Con pointed out.

"Since when's what you do fair?"

Con smirked. "Since now. And you have no idea what I do."

"Hustler with a conscience. Interesting."

Yeah, it was interesting all right. "I'll meet you two exits down the highway."

Quinn raised a brow but didn't say anything.

Con wanted to be annoyed, but he was too busy noticing the tattoos that snaked out from under Quinn's pushed-up shirtsleeves, and one that twined elegantly along the side of Quinn's neck. "Seriously. Don't wait here for me. I'll be fine. Trust me."

Quinn looked between Con and the pool table and gave a soft snort in retort.

Quinn didn't listen to Con's orders, mainly because he didn't take them, not that he didn't believe Con could handle himself. When Con readied to leave, Quinn saw three of the men follow him out. Quinn brought up the rear, walked out onto the dark sidewalk in time to see Con smoothly dispatching the three men, doing barely any damage, but enough to make the men go back inside the bar.

For reinforcements, Quinn figured.

"Ready?" Con called as he got on his Harley, which was parked two spaces over from Quinn's big truck.

"Do we have a choice?" Quinn asked as he started his truck.

Con laughed, a sound that carried over the roar of his own bike. "Unless you want to deal with more of them. I'm happy to do it."

Fuck. Not especially. Was it going to be like this for the entire trip, getting Con's ass out of scrapes?

"You weren't supposed to wait," Con called to him, right before he pulled out into the road. Quinn followed close behind, the two vehicles taking off smoothly into the night and disappearing without anyone following them.

They'd gotten lucky. Quinn knew that. He could only imagine the amount of times a trail of cars had followed Con.

Finally, he pulled off the exit, behind Con, as planned. They parked along the side of the rest stop where they'd have a good view if anyone drove in. It was mainly truckers stopping here this time of night anyway.

Con got off the bike and strolled up to Quinn's truck. Quinn opened the door and slid down to meet him. "What would you do if I wasn't here?"

Con laughed, sounding slightly crazy "What? You think I need you to bodyguard me? Newsflash—I don't."

"Fine. So we ride together and go our separate ways at night. You can hustle pool and defend your own honor."

"While you rest your old man bones? Sounds good."

"Let's leave my bone out of it," Quinn growled. Con looked right between his legs, letting his gaze linger, then slowly let it drift up to Quinn's face.

God, this fucker needed to be taught a lesson and Quinn was itching to do that, wanted to take him over his lap and...

Con grinned, like he knew what Quinn was thinking. Which wasn't possible. He was military, not psychic.

"We're not doing that every night," Quinn informed him.

"Last I looked, this wasn't a military base and you aren't in charge of me," Con told him.

Quinn raised a brow. "You're looking for someone to take charge?"

Con hesitated for only the briefest second. "Did I say that?"

Well, he might as well have, because dammit, Con was

screaming for someone—the right someone—to hold him down and fuck him.

But he was supposed to simply be taking a road trip to see Scott. With Con. "Escorting him," was how Scott termed it. As he put it, "Without you, Con would eventually make it here, probably with a police car in tow."

Quinn glanced at Con. "Doesn't the military have rules?"

"Lots of them. Be specific."

"Moral ones? Propriety."

Con snorted. Motioned to himself. "Not in uniform, right? And I don't see any MPs around. Dude, I'm free. And you're killing my buzz."

Quinn's buzz was nonexistent, unless he counted the low-level buzz in his head that made him want to strangle Con and take him in hand in equal parts, and *fuck*, that wasn't good.

Instead, he went back to the truck, grabbed the itinerary that was Con's and handed it to him.

Con began to flip through it, standing under the lights of the Arby's in back of him. "Looks like our tour guide/travel agent took care of everything."

"Yeah, these came this morning." Quinn had glanced through the itinerary briefly. "It's got both weeks planned, down to the hotels he's reserved and paid for."

Con sighed and stuffed the folder in his bag. "Are we set for tonight?"

"Hotel's an hour away."

"We're starting tonight?"

"According to Mr. Control Freak, yes." He glanced at Con's bike. "Want to stow this? I've got a cover for it."

"You ride?"

"S'why I bought this truck." He opened the flatbed and

pulled the ramp down. Con wheeled the bike up easily, chained it in and covered it up.

Then he joined Quinn in the cab, sliding into the passenger's side and dumping his camouflage duffel behind the seat. "She ride well?"

"Not bad. Better since I played with her."

"Gearheads," Con muttered, but he nodded with a smile when Quinn started the motor and it rumbled to life with a resounding roar.

Neither one of them was very talkative. They were both wound up from that last minute burst of adrenaline, and Quinn just wanted to get to the hotel before he lost that charge. With the radio pulsing some old school heavy metal—music Con didn't object to—Quinn tried to figure out the suddenly compliant soldier sitting next to him.

Scott'd never mentioned Con being gay or bi and it was obviously possible that he'd had no idea. Between DADT—because repealed or not it'd still been a part of Con's military life at one point—and the fact that these men were in one of the most gay-unfriendly professions, Quinn couldn't blame Con for not discussing his personal life.

Con didn't seem like he was the type to hide what he was, though. At least not off-base. While he could easily pass for straight, Quinn noted that, at least tonight, Con had made sure to catch as many men's eyes as he could.

Granted, Quinn had never come out and told Scott he was gay. He figured his family hadn't been able to handle the fact that he wasn't enlisting, and being gay would throw them over the edge. It wasn't a reveal he deemed necessary.

And the Dom part? Yeah, no fucking way.

Maybe he'd read Con's vibe wrong but, but...yeah, no. Especially not when Con had given him that smile and boldly looked him up and down.

Hell, had Scott known about him and told Con? Was this some kind of weird set-up?

Granted, if it was, Con had seemed as clueless about it as Quinn'd been. At some point, Con had started looking through the itinerary again. "Christ, he turned this into a military op."

"That he did."

"Well, this is what he wanted. Can't not comply with his wishes now," Con pointed out.

Two weeks. "Think we can make it in one?"

"And hit all the hotspots he highlighted?" Con shook his head. "What's the rush? I'm making the most of this—I plan to have fun in as many states as I can."

Jesus. Quinn rubbed his forehead. Nothing about this trip was fun, especially the endpoint. There was still time to say "fuck it," to get on a plane and show up, and hell, what was Scott going to do? Send him back to gather up Con? The guy was a grown fucking man in the Army, for Christsakes—he could get himself across the country.

And if he couldn't? Well, then maybe Con had bigger problems than Quinn should be expected to handle.

By the time Quinn pulled the truck into the hotel's lot, it was close to three in the morning. Con let him check them in, take the keys, sign for the room, and then Con followed him into the elevator.

The room was a two-bedroom suite. Con walked toward the room to the left immediately.

"We'll sleep in today and travel through late afternoon. We'll get to the next stop before nine tomorrow night and we'll be back on Scott's schedule," Quinn said firmly. Con grunted, went through the connecting doors ("Without shared suites you'll never keep track of him," were Scott's instructions) and left the door open.

Quinn glanced into Con's room and saw the man's clothes in a trail leading to the bed. And Con was only under the sheet —really, only partially under—and very obviously naked.

And there was no ink on his body at all—at least from what Quinn could see, which was three quarters of a solid body. That was a shame, because Con really had the perfect contours.

Stop thinking about his contours, Quinn.

But he couldn't stop. These next weeks would no doubt be a crash course in everything Con. And what an education it would be, if tonight was any indication.

And since his mind was racing, he did what he always did when he needed to calm the fuck down—he sketched.

He'd been born with art in his blood, and he'd been sketching from the time he could hold a pencil. He'd also liked giving orders. "Bossy as fuck," his father would say. "He'll make a good general."

He glanced back and forth between the bed and the paper in front of him, drawing freehand...and feeling oddly freer than he had in a long damned time.

INKED: THIRDS

INKED #2

Book 2 in the Inked Series, on sale now!

For Aleks, the third time wasn't the charm...and fighting for survival was only the beginning...

Aleks is a tattoo artist at Inked. He's also a man with a troubled history and a future bent on vengeance. But his plans for revenge are derailed when he meets a man with ties to his past. A man who also holds a promise of the future.

Brogan is dangerous for Aleks in more ways than one. He's former military, a successful businessman and a strong hand in the bedroom—everything Aleks wants, under the worst possible circumstances. It's up to Aleks to figure out what—and who—is worth fighting for.

Enjoy the first chapter from THIRDS:

Present day

Brogan was finally back home from his extended European stay—six months when he'd only meant to hang out with some friends for a couple of months—and decided to catch up on his real estate holdings. He was lucky enough to have the wealth and a family name behind him that allowed him to travel the way he did, but he also continued to work from abroad.

Brogan preferred the real estate market, with its highs and lows, to the banality of the canning factories and the like that his great-grandfather had established. Without them, there would be no Montgomery-Johnstone money to invest. Because of it, Brogan was able to make himself wealthier.

Still, he sat on the board of directors, the monthly meetings with his cousin Harry and the other men in suits always an experience he wished he didn't have to repeat. Although he'd grown up with Harry, the distance between them couldn't be more apparent.

He had managers and landlords handling the properties, but he liked to keep up with his buildings in person when he could, in case there were any complaints he could rectify. He'd discovered that most people were more reasonable if they thought they were tugging an owner's ear.

He was also a good landlord, and he'd saved his favorite shop for last, a tattoo parlor called Inked. When the building manager originally brought him the lease from the new clients, Brogan had gone to meet with them. One of the men was military, both had solid credit and Brogan knew a good tattoo parlor fit the neighborhood perfectly.

It turned out his hunch was more than right. Each year, the tattoo shop was featured in papers and online for its gifted artists, many of them visiting, since Quinn brought in the artists who'd done his tattoos.

Today, when Brogan pushed open the glass doors, everyone looked over...except the dark-haired man giving a tattoo in the center of the large room.

"Brogan, good to see you again." Quinn, co-owner of the shop and a master tattooer himself came over, hand extended.

"Welcome back, man." Con, his partner—in business and life—came up next and punched him in the shoulder. Quinn's father and brother had served, and Con was former military like Brogan, and he was more than happy to be renting to other vets. They were great tenants, and they were renting the majority of the building out, since Con decided that he also wanted the apartments above the shop so he wouldn't have to, in his words, "commute."

As Brogan got to know them, he quickly realized that although Quinn would often roll his eyes at Con, he also gave in to most of his whims. If Brogan could find someone to make him a quarter as happy, he'd be more than fine with that. "Thanks. Sorry I was gone so long. I'm assuming everything's okay over here?"

"More than," Quinn assured him. "We're still taking bets on when you'll get your first ink."

"Sorry, still not my thing." Brogan's eyes flicked to the man in the shop who most definitely *was*. "You've gotten some fresh faces in here."

"Yeah, we took on a couple of new artists. Becca does piercings and Aleks over there does fantastic pieces." Quinn motioned to the man Brogan had noticed.

Aleks's head had been down as he concentrated. It still was but he raised his chin a bit, enough to make Brogan start.

Because it was *him*, the fighter Brogan had been picturing

for what seemed like forever. The image of his sweat-slicked body had gotten Brogan through the worst of Special Forces training, the small piece of comfort he'd allowed himself in those few moments of stolen downtime. He'd used the fighter's image to motivate him, to turn him on, to prove he was still alive when he felt dead inside.

10 years earlier

"Gotta show you a good time before you head back into hell," his cousin, Harry, had told him, then ushered him into an underground basement.

This was so far from the good time Brogan planned on having for himself later, in another type of club in another part of the city, but for now, he humored his cousin. Harry liked to act the part of the big spender, which was lost on Brogan, since they shared the same family fortune.

Harry thought Brogan was slumming it in the military. Thought he was crazy to put himself through the gauntlet of Special Forces training, but Brogan could never have done the fraternity shit that he'd been hearing Harry brag about for years.

"We're here for the first fight of the night." Harry handed him a cold beer and pointed to the ring inside the steel cage. The crowd surrounded it, standing outside the chain link as though watching some kind of exotic animals through the metal.

The first guy was shoved into the ring and looked back at the man who'd pushed him out there. He was big and the jeers from he crowd had him giving everyone his middle finger and sneering.

Great. A bunch of overgrown college kids trying to pay their way through school, according to Harry.

But Brogan soon forgot about not wanting to be there when the first guy walked into the ring, escorted by his coach, and was locked inside with an ominously loud clink of a lock clicking into place.

No way out. *Brogan's skin itched as though he was the one trapped.*

The guy had dark hair and hypnotically dark eyes. He scanned the crowd, wearing only blue shorts and white tape on his hands.

"Money on the fighter in blue," his cousin told the man who came around to collect the bets.

"He's favored," the man confirmed, handed them their chits.

Yeah, I favor him.

When the fight began Aleks moved like a blur—fast, slick with sweat and yeah, Brogan had his jack-off material for a good while. The other men in his bunk would be thinking about breasts and Brogan would be dreaming about bringing this fighter to his knees, putting his cock in his mouth, watching him submit.

And now, his fantasy was in front of him, alive and well and tattooing a barrel-chested men on his wide biceps. Concentrating fully on the picture taking shape under his gun, the black and gray ink he constantly wiped away revealing a perfect symbol, a cross with a military insignia above it, an intricate, original design.

Damn, the guy still looked the same. Better, actually. His face was chiseled and matured—model material—his body still muscled but a fighter's muscles.

Aleks didn't have the tattoos back then that Brogan noted running down his arms—he'd only worn blue shorts, so Brogan would've seen them if he had.

Con clapped him on the shoulder and prompted, "Sure you're not in the market for a tattoo?"

Con's brow arched and there was no mistaking his intention. Everyone noticed the way Brogan watched Aleks...except maybe Aleks himself. "I'm in the market, but not for one of my own," Brogan told him.

Con smiled broadly. "Brogan, I like the way you think."

"That's seriously perfect," the Army vet in Aleks's chair breathed as he stared at the complicated 82nd Airborne symbol on his biceps. It was shaded black and gray with a 3-D look to it. Aleks had helped him pick the perfect spot to highlight it best, using the natural shape of his muscle.

"Looks good on you," Aleks confirmed.

"You serve?"

"No. One of the guys who owns this place did," Aleks said. "I just have the respect and appreciation."

"It shows." The vet shook his hand and gave Aleks the once-over. "I'll be back for another one soon, I'm sure."

"I'll be here," Aleks told him.

The vet glanced back at Aleks as he walked away and Aleks moved to clean his equipment. Tattooing—and being tattooed—was a personal thing, a vulnerable thing, and a lot of times feelings and emotions came out that weren't necessarily the person's true feelings.

This customer's reaction was a product of that—he was straight, Aleks knew, but sometimes after sitting in a chair and getting close the way they had...well, things could feel different. Because of that, Aleks got hit on a lot—men and women alike, young and old. He just seemed to have a magnetic pull. At least that's what lovers had told him.

Probably because he was unavailable. His life was devoted to two things: tattooing and taking down the man who'd ruined both his life and Vann's.

Vann had exacted his own revenge on both their accounts, and he'd found a way back. Aleks was happy for him. He knew he'd never get that far if he didn't exact his own revenge. He stayed up nights, planning. Waiting. And the perfect opportunity would present itself, where the guy wouldn't be surrounded by bodyguards. It was only a matter of time.

But when Brogan Montgomery-Johnstone walked into the tattoo parlor, Aleks was so fucking unprepared, he didn't know if he should walk out the back door or right up into Brogan's face. Because time? It might be up.

He looked just like Aleks remembered—a little older. Tanned. Blond, blue-eyed, All-American and handsome as fuck. His bearing was military and if Aleks closed his eyes, he could picture that night, making fast work of one of his first opponents in the ring while Brogan watched him intently.

Sometimes the fights made Aleks hard—a purely physical reaction his body had to fighting—but that night, it had been all about Brogan's intense stare. If Aleks hadn't been locked back into his cell afterward, he might've left the cage and gone with Brogan somewhere to get fucked.

Now, Brogan's eyes caught and held his, and yes, Brogan remembered him, let it show for a long moment before putting on his "all business" face again for Aleks's bosses.

Aleks would've been content for Brogan to finish up his talk and leave, but Con put a kink in that plan by calling out, "Hey Aleks, come meet Brogan. He owns the building."

And Aleks couldn't refuse that, so he ambled over to reach out and take Brogan's outstretched hand in his. He wasn't a big believer in the whole "bolt of lightning when you meet the right guy" crap, but hell, a shot of electricity seemed to jolt a current through both of them. For a second, they just stared at each other; probably equal parts shock and lust were unmistakable on his face the way they were on Brogan's.

Even if Aleks hadn't recognized him from the fights, he would've from the pictures he'd found of Brogan's cousin, Harry. Aka the man Aleks had marked for death. So far, Aleks had been able to rule out Brogan's direct involvement in funding the fight club, barring the fact that he shared the same last name and part of a vast family fortune with Harry.

Harry was a major backer—the biggest fish—in the death-matches. Rumor had it that Harry was the one who'd come up with the concept. As for the whys? That probably could've broken Aleks more easily than any fight ever had if he allowed himself to dwell on it: for *sport*. Harry was rich, bored, looking for easy entertainment for his wealthy and out-of-town clients.

It was also a front for the Russian mob.

And now Harry's cousin was standing right in front of him, like a package with a bow on top.

Leverage.

"Brogan Montgomery-Johnstone's a big deal in this community," Con told him after Brogan had said goodbye...reluctantly, it seemed to Aleks.

"So I've heard," he said dryly. "Was I supposed to kiss his bare feet when he walked in? Or lick his boots first?"

Con shrugged. "Hell, if you're into that, I'm sure he'd be all right with it." When Aleks narrowed his eyes at him, Con explained, "Rumor has it he's a Dom."

Ah, now *that* made a hell of a lot of sense. His body seemed to want to respond to Brogan with a ferocity Aleks wasn't used to. "I'm not in the market for one."

"Hey, don't knock it if you haven't tried it."

Aleks had tried it. Liked it too, just not enough to have one permanently attached to him. To many fucking rules, too much *yes sir* and *no sir* for his tastes. He'd watched the scene, didn't mind playing, but any relationship didn't sound great to him. Getting close to anyone wasn't on his to-do list. He had Vann and now Con and Quinn, who were cool and looked after him.

He told Con, "I've got all the entanglements I can handle at the moment."

"Famous last words," Quinn murmured as he came up to claim Con and rescue Aleks.

Quinn guided Con upstairs to their apartment. They really had taken over the majority of the building, and although they lived together it was nice that they had a space to live and a separate place to play, complete with Con's pool table.

"Think I freaked Aleks out?" Con asked, the smirk still on his face.

"Maybe a little. He and Brogan had some serious chemistry going," Quinn said, stretching out his shoulder a little—he'd had a long week of tattooing. "A blind man could've seen it."

Con moved to stand behind him and began to rub his shoulder. "Now it's up to Aleks to do something about it. Nab himself a rich man."

"Right. Just like you found your sugar daddy?" Quinn teased, then groaned as Con hit the right spot.

"No joke—I did," Con snarked, then got serious. "Aleks is quiet. A good guy. Quiet."

"You said that," Quinn pointed out.

"Bears repeating. Quiet equals dangerous. Guy's definitely dangerous."

"To who?"

"Anyone he considers an enemy."

Quinn looked over his shoulder and blinked. "Glad we're not on that list."

Con murmured against his cheek, "I'm definitely not. But don't worry, *daddy*—I'll protect you."

"You definitely need a beating."

Con smiled. "And you're just the man to give it to me. So what are you waiting for?"

MEN OF HONOR: BOUND BY HONOR

MEN OF HONOR #1

Don't miss the Men of Honor!
BOUND BY HONOR:
Book 1 in the Men of Honor Series, on sale now!

A promise forces two men to bare themselves...completely.

One year ago on a mission gone wrong, Tanner James failed to save the life of Jesse, his Army Ranger teammate. Before dying in that South American jungle, Jesse extracted a promise that won't let Tanner rest until it's fulfilled—no matter what it costs him.

Damon Price loved Jesse, but problems in their relationship had come to a head right before Jesse left on his final mission. Now a reluctant Dom and a man still in mourning, he's not happy when Tanner appears at his BDSM club. And even less happy with Jesse's last request—that Tanner sub for him for one night.

After a rough start, Damon realizes that the tough soldier, despite his protests, aches for someone to take control. And

Tanner senses a hesitance, an insecurity in Damon that makes him wonder if he's simply a placeholder for Jesse, or if their tentative connection could grow into something more.

For Jesse's sake, they agree to try one weekend together. Then duty calls, and a series of attacks that have been happening near the club hits too close to home, making both men wonder if giving their hearts is a maneuver fraught with too much risk...

Warning: Contains rough language, rougher sex and warriors who fall hard for each other.

Chapter One from *Bound By Honor*:

Tanner James had been to hell and back more times than he could count over the course of his twenty- six years and was always pretty sure he'd live to make the trip again. But this time, even as adrenaline raced through his body and every muscle tensed for battle, hell beckoned with a one-way ticket and without a goddamned firefight in sight.

No, that would've been easier, *much* easier than this slow crawl to the door of Crave—a BDSM club with the reputation of being both accessible and safe—the week before Christmas.

He looked up at the dark sign with white lettering at the entrance and thought about turning back and going home.

If he hadn't promised Jesse that he'd do this, that he'd look up Jesse's former boyfriend, he'd be home right now, having just returned from a month-long mission, not about to offer himself up like some bondage sacrifice.

This wasn't his scene. Not really. He was all about rough sex, was bisexual with a definite preference to men for as long as he could remember, used to having to *don't ask, don't tell*, thanks to his military career—but this? Having to go in and greet the owner with a message from his dead lover? Well, that was fucking weird and could get him thrown out on his ass.

Jesus Christ, this was going to suck.

The man checking patrons who entered was dressed in bright, loud colors. Tight black leather pants. Guyliner. And he flirted in an over-the-top manner with anyone he deemed hot enough.

Tanner knew he'd be the subject of the man's flirtation. Although he'd shrugged it off his entire life, the looks and stares and come-ons he'd been on the receiving end of forever told him he was handsome.

He was more interested in being the best Army Ranger he could, spent most days knee-deep in jungle crap with paint on his face and men who only cared that he could shoot an M-14 with dizzying accuracy.

"Hey."

"Hello, gorgeous. Please tell me you're alone." The man peeked behind Tanner, saw no one and clapped his hands. "Alone. There is a God."

"I'm looking for Damon Price."

"I'll bet you are," the man said with a shake of his head. "Shame, really, that they all want what they can't have."

"I just need to talk to him."

The man erupted into peals of girlish laughter and Tanner rolled his eyes. He'd never been into queens and this was why. If he was going to fuck a man, he was going to fuck a man. "Tell him I've got a message from Jesse."

The man stopped, nearly choked, but before he could answer, he was elbowed out of the way by a much taller blond man—ruggedly handsome although unsmiling, and Tanner wondered if he was face to face with Damon himself.

But rather than introduce himself, he asked, "What did you say about Jesse?"

"You heard me," Tanner bit out.

The man nodded slowly. "I heard you. I just don't know how Damon's going to feel about this." He paused. "Are you sure you want to go there?"

Tanner reacted before he could stop himself. "Why the *fuck* would you care where I want to go?"

The man raised a brow and held up a finger, indicating for Tanner to wait a minute, before disappearing down a back hallway.

Last chance to head for the hills. And despite the ease with which he could do so, Tanner remained rooted in place.

He couldn't see very far into the club at all from where he stood—it was designed purposely to let the incoming patrons hear the familiar sounds of sex occasionally rising over the music. The smell of sex was also unmistakable, partially hidden and mixed with whiskey and smoke. It was meant to beckon, to lead men astray...and Tanner didn't bother to hide his hard-on.

A few minutes later, Tanner was being led by the blond man who introduced himself as LC back to a private office with a big *Do Not Disturb* sign on the door.

No doubt, *this* counted as disturbing Damon, but it had been eating away at Tanner for a year now. He had to rid himself of this burden, do what Jesse asked and then go home and pretend none of it ever happened.

Before going in, he glanced at his watch. Just after midnight. Exactly the way Jesse had wanted it.

A hard growl of a voice called, "Come in."

LC stared at him, and Tanner, in turn, stared at the floor for a long moment. And then he opened the door and realized he'd been anything but prepared for Damon Price. Tanner was big and broad and strong, stood six foot three and turned heads wherever he went. But Damon—he was well over six foot five, with jet black hair and chiseled features. He stood, hands at his sides in a deceptively casual stance, dressed in full black leather and looking like a fucking badass.

Tanner nearly hyperventilated, because Jesse hadn't mentioned this part.

"He's my boyfriend and he owns a club," was all Jesse said. *"He's strong—reminds me of you. He's a Dom."*

"I'm not a Dom."

"No. But you could probably use one. It would be the only kind of man who could handle you."

Jesse had closed his eyes then before Tanner could tell him he had no interest in being anyone's bottom boy. Because Jesse had been talking to him about boyfriends and Doms when he'd been dying, slowly and painfully in the middle of a jungle in South America where he and his Ranger team had been on a mission, and Tanner had been fucking helpless to stop it.

Fuck.

He shoved his hands in his pockets so Damon wouldn't see the fists he couldn't uncurl and hoped the pain didn't show in his eyes.

This was supposed to bring closure—to both Damon and Tanner. There was no way to break a promise to a dead man.

Damon studied him for a few minutes. Tanner wasn't the type to squirm and he wasn't about to start now. Finally, the man said, "I hear you have a message from Jesse. And I swear to Christ, if you're fucking with me, I'll put your head through the wall."

Tanner snorted in spite of himself. "Okay, sure. I'd like to see you try."

Damon pushed away from the desk and stood toe-to-toe with him. "Talk."

Talk. Yeah, like it was that easy. "Jesse told me to come here —to ask for you. To tell you that..." Fuck. He shifted, aware that the proximity of Damon was freaking him out. If he hadn't been Jesse's, Tanner might've made a move without a second thought.

As if he knew what he was thinking, Damon arched an eyebrow at him, his lip curled into a half sneer.

Fuck it all. "I'm supposed to tell you to have a session with me. Jesse wanted it that way." "A session?" Damon repeated.

"Yeah. I'm supposed to let you Dom me. It was Jesse's dying wish."

Damon paled, took a step back from Tanner, and then another. "Is this a sick joke?"

"Do I look like I'm joking?"

"You little fuck." Damon had Tanner's shirt bunched in his fists, was slamming him against the office wall hard. "You sick bastard. You think you can ingratiate yourself to me by using Jesse?"

Tanner ground his teeth together hard and tamped back his anger. He'd known Damon wouldn't take this well. If Tanner had been in the same position, he doubted he would either. "He asked me to wait a year before I came here. He died after midnight."

"How do you know that?" Damon demanded. "Even I don't know that."

No, he wouldn't. The mission was deemed classified—and Jesse's time of death a closely guarded secret. "I was with him when he died."

Damon let out a long, hissing breath and let go of Tanner's shirt.

"I'm sorry—I didn't know how else to tell you. Jesse made me promise—"

"Stop saying his name," Damon growled hoarsely.

"He made me promise I'd wait the year. Said you wouldn't be ready before that. That you'd need to be dragged back into the land of the living, kicking and screaming. He said to tell you...to use the skull- and-crossbones collar with the broken latch." He spoke fast, stopped to catch his breath at the end. Gauged Damon's reaction.

The man hadn't moved a muscle during Tanner's speech. Simply stared, and Tanner tensed more, wondering if he was going to have to fight tonight.

Fighting and fucking were definitely two of his favorite things to do, sometimes all in the same night—or hour—or hell, the same time, but he had a feeling that he'd be pushing his luck taking on this guy.

He was in way over his head. And he couldn't remember the last time—if ever—he'd felt that way.

Damon's features relaxed slightly. He sat back on the top of the desk, folded his arms and stared Tanner up and down. A hard, assessing stare that was enough to make Tanner hard with desire and anticipation.

He wasn't sure why the sudden thought of Damon taking him got him hot, but that was short-lived, because he saw the tension in Damon's stance, the pain in his eyes. Tanner wanted to apologize, but he wasn't sure what for. Wanted to tell Damon that he was scared to fucking death that the Domming would actually happen—and also scared that it wouldn't.

He was so fucked up he could barely see straight.

Damon finally spoke. "I wouldn't touch you. You're not man

enough to handle me."

Jesse's words echoed in Tanner's ear. *It would be the only kind of man who could handle you.*

Tanner hadn't been able to handle a relationship—or being touched, really, since what happened to Jesse last year. And so he nodded and he said, "You're right about that. This was a mistake."

The failure hanging on him heavily, he pushed out the door, went through the club and headed for the parking lot.

Jesse.

Damon had mourned over that man, cried over him, beat his fists against the wall, up until three months earlier. Things had eased, but he still wore the cloak of grief that sometimes threatened to choke him.

Now was one of those times. He'd waited until the gorgeous man left his office before he fell apart and tried his best not to hyperventilate.

Use the skull-and-crossbones collar with the broken latch.

The boy who'd just left his office would have no way of knowing that—wouldn't have known that Damon kept that collar in his loft, had fixed the latch right after Jesse died because it was one of the only things he could do.

Damon wouldn't be able to use the damned collar on this boy—Jesse knew that collaring meant something—that it didn't happen on a first night together.

You don't even know the boy's name.

He shuddered involuntarily that he'd thought of him as *the boy*. Because that's what he'd called Jesse—and only Jesse.

Jesse had been the first to ever thaw what Damon had considered a heart of ice. First, and the *only*.

But something tugged at his gut.

He could've been lying. This could be part of an elaborate scam.

The only thing was, the man had definitely been military. A Ranger, like Jesse, or so he said. Damon didn't doubt it, had a nose for those things, having been in special forces himself what seemed like a lifetime ago. And the timing was exactly right. Jesse had died a year ago, nearly to the hour, although he'd lied to the boy about not having that information.

Fuck.

He called through the open office door, "LC, grab that guy who just left."

"I'm not your bitch," LC drawled, and no, LC was no one's bitch...not since Styx left. "And he's already in the lot."

"Dammit."

LC held his gaze for a second and then called to one of the bodyguards. "Renn—grab the guy in the brown leather jacket who just left. And bring a few guys—he won't come willingly."

LC didn't say anything more, didn't have to, and just headed to the front of the club to supervise. And Damon waited in his office, trying not to pace. Trying not to picture what the boy would look like, bound and spread for him.

Trying to pretend he wasn't hard at the thought of it.

He shifted but could do nothing to hide the erection in the pants he wore, and when LC barged back into the office, it was the first thing he noticed.

Thankfully, he didn't comment on it, just said, "They've got him and he's not happy."

"Makes two of us."

"Did he really know Jesse?"

Damon nodded. "He says that Jesse sent him here—wanted him to have a session with me."

LC's eyes widened, but wisely his mouth remained closed. He was part owner of Crave, working mainly behind the scenes.

He was also Damon's best friend—the only person Damon confided everything in. The only one he trusted enough to let him run the business in those months after Jesse died, when Damon couldn't get out of bed most days. LC had finally gotten him up and functioning.

Just then, the boy was dragged back in by three men—he was pissed for sure, but not fighting as hard as he could. Damon knew that, and whether it was grief or curiosity or both, he couldn't tell yet.

"Let him go," Damon commanded, and the men dropped him and left the room with LC, the office door shutting behind them as the boy stumbled forward until Damon caught him, held him hard by the biceps and stared at him again.

He was handsome as hell—all-American-looking, a blond haired, blue-eyed devil, even with his lips twisted into an angry grimace.

"What the fuck do you think you're doing?" The boy jerked out of his grasp and yes, he was strong. Damon had suspected as much. Earlier, when Damon had him by the shirt, backed against the wall, he hadn't flinched. It was the calm of a man who knew how to fight—who knew how to kill.

"What's your name?"

A jut of a chin, a glint of wild eyes and he ground out, "Tanner."

"Why did you come here?"

"Because I made a promise to Jesse when he was dying. I don't break promises like that."

"And you're willing to follow through on what he wanted."

Tanner pressed his lips together—he wanted to say no, that much Damon knew. For some reason, this handsome, strong, brave man wanted nothing to do with being Dommed, and it didn't appear to be for the usual reasons.

No, he wasn't uncomfortable, either in this club or with Damon and his leathers. But something was most definitely wrong with him.

"I'll do what Jesse wanted, yes."

"But you don't think you're man enough."

He waited for Tanner to snap an answer back, but none came. Instead, he shrugged.

"Well then, there's no time like the present. But no collar." He motioned for Tanner to follow him, out the door of the office, down a small hallway and into a room marked Room Four.

Once inside, Damon pressed a few buttons to bring the lights up and to remove the shading from the plate-glass divider that separated the room from the rest of the club.

As soon as he did so, the bar began to cheer. Damon activated the two-way speakers as well, so the sounds went from muffled to completely clear.

Tanner's eyes widened. "We're doing this here—where everyone can see?"

"Yes. That's what Jesse would've wanted."

Tanner couldn't have known that was the furthest thing from the truth—that Jesse understood the value of privacy at the start of a D/s relationship.

That Jesse would hate him for this.

Well, Damon hated Jesse for dying and leaving him. For refusing to quit the military and let Damon take care of him for the rest of his life.

For recognizing that Damon had been slowly dying inside during the last year of their relationship and continuing to satisfy his own needs instead.

Tanner swallowed hard and then he nodded.

Yes, let's see if this man is for real.

MEN OF HONOR: BOUND BY LAW

BOOK 2 IN THE MEN OF HONOR SERIES

Law Connor is about to come face to face with the man he can't forget...and the one man who's in danger of remembering everything...

Enjoy the following excerpt from *Bound by Law*:

Paulo wasn't taking no for an answer, so Law had no choice but to concede to having dinner with the man. He was getting past the anonymous fucking stage with Paulo and Paulo knew that, took advantage of him when he was weak from orgasms. Hence, the fancy goddamned dinner at an expensive restaurant where the detective obviously knew the staff. They gave the men a private table in the back, and appetizers began arriving without them having to place any orders. Paulo kept filling up his wine glass and Law got looser with each glass, and he knew he'd be going home with Paulo again that night for sure. Or maybe he'd take Paulo back to his new apartment for the first time, a new place, a fresh start...the same guy more than once, and that was a fucking record that had remained unbroken for ten years.

"Tell me what LC stands for," Paulo murmured now. "Or I'll tie you down and fuck it out of you."

"That's incentive to tell you?" LC asked as he scanned his menu for the main courses, not wanting to let Paulo see how turned on he got when Paulo spoke like that. Because he did so easily, his eyes hot, and LC remembered how good his body had felt against the younger man's.

Before last night, it had been over a month since he'd seen him last. Paulo had come to visit him in the hospital after LC thwarted an attacker who'd been hurting men outside Crave, his BDSM club. Before that, Paulo had given him a gift—a gift certificate, to be exact—for a tattoo, which LC hadn't used yet. Paulo's torso was close to being covered with them, intricate designs that swirled over muscles in his chest, back and arms and made him that much goddamned harder to resist.

LC loved looking at them, loved tracing them with his tongue, his fingers, watching the way they moved when LC was pounding him, the way he had last night.

"I was glad you came over," Paulo said after they'd finished the appetizers and waited on the next course.

LC had been surprised, too. He'd been driving around restlessly, because Damon was holed up with Tanner and prowling the club scene no longer held his interest. Crave was sold and things were moving forward.

Everyone was moving forward and he'd been standing still. At first, there had been a lot to do with the sale of the club and the lofts and the construction of the new apartments he and Damon bought, along with the rest of the building. They were now living on opposite ends of the top floor, and the plan was to renovate and rent the rest of the apartments.

There was a hell of a lot to do, but LC didn't feel like handling any of it, especially not last night. No, he'd wanted to handle someone, and his car had pointed in the direction of Paulo's place almost as if he'd had no control.

But LC knew that was bullshit.

Paulo had barely been able to get out a hello before LC had him pinned, telling Paulo he'd been dreaming about him before he could stop himself. After that, it was a blur of hands and tongues and *oh yeah*s, and then LC was agreeing to dinner, because he'd just taken the man without so much as a this-is-where-I've-been-for-the-past-month explanation.

He'd stayed through until the sun came up and straggled back to his new place, and now he was here, next to this man in this dark restaurant, and he'd been turned on from the time Paulo picked him up.

If he was honest with himself, Paulo was handling him and he really fucking liked it.

Paulo hadn't asked him any more about the dreams LC had about him, and for that, LC was grateful. Because this, the tug in the stomach when Paulo looked at him, was new...the first time since Styx, and he knew this man could make him happy, if he allowed it.

He downed the rest of his wine and stood before he told Paulo that. "Headed to the restroom—I'll be back."

"I'd join you, but I have a reputation in this place," Paulo said with a sly smile.

"I'm sure." LC threaded his way through the back hallway, found the men's room. He pissed and washed up in the private restroom, wiped his hands on a paper towel, and it was all normal. So *normal*.

Until the lights went out and shots rang out inside the restaurant and an arm came up across his body, a hand over his mouth, and his natural instinct to fight like hell was quelled with a single breath.

Styx. He'd recognize the man's scent—his touch—blind-folded. Many a time he'd actually done so, but this situation was a thousand percent different.

"Not a word." Styx's voice, rough like gravel. Rougher when he was angry or aroused. His breath was warm and minty—Altoids. The man had always been addicted to them.

Damn, you remembered the oddest things when your ass was on the line. And speaking of asses, his was pressed hard to Styx's groin...and the man's arousal was unmistakable. Nice to know he wasn't the only one affected by the close proximity.

He moved his head and Styx took his hand away.

"Paulo," he said, and Styx answered, "Your friend's safe—my associate has him."

Good, that was good, but Jesus, what was going on here?

He heard the slight snick of a gun's safety being release and then heavy footsteps. Whoever was coming wasn't interested in stealth.

Not good.

"Whatever happens, stay put in here. I'll take care of every-thing." Styx barely mouthed the words but LC heard them loud and clear. And then he was left alone in the dark, and yeah, the metaphor of his goddamned life with and without Styx, and he listened and waited.

No more shots, but someone had died. LC had been around stealth and death long enough in the Army to the point where he could taste the violence. He'd been on the receiving end of it since birth.

Goddammit, Law, shake that shit off.

And then Styx was back, tugging at him, and LC resisted.

"I'm not going anywhere until you tell me what the hell's going on out there."

"Someone died. Now shut up and do what I say."

"I'm so beyond listening to you."

"Law, you have no idea who and what you're up against. Come with me," Styx said, and LC reluctantly followed him into the restaurant's storeroom, close to the parking lot. And even though it was dark as night inside the restaurant's back room, LC would know the man, could practically see the dark blond hair, longer than it had been, eyes that never failed to mesmerize him, the hard body and even harder cock that probed him earlier.

Law knew what he was up against—and he was powerless to stop it. And when he started to push past Styx, Styx let him go at first and then pushed him hard against the wall by the door.

"Are you with that guy?" he whispered into LC's neck, and he wanted to tell Styx not to do that.

Instead, he ground out, "His name is Paulo. And now you're worried about my dating habits?"

"I'm always worried about you."

"The not calling or writing is a great way to show that."

"It's the way it has to be."

Has to be...not using the past tense meant that's what would happen after Styx did whatever it was he needed to here. "What, exactly, is happening out there to get the CIA involved?"

"Can't tell you."

"Right. I don't have the clearance to be involved in any part of your life." Never did. Never would. "Let fucking go of me."

"You can't leave now."

"Then you'll have to arrest me."

With that, Styx reached up and yanked LC's arms down and

behind his back, and when the cuffs snicked on his wrists, he cursed bitterly. "Where's Paulo?"

"Safe."

"Not what I asked."

"Are you two serious?"

"Why don't you tell me? You've been spying on me for God knows how long." "I call it keeping you safe."

"Get. The fuck. Off me."

Styx didn't listen. Never did, which was why the military hadn't been for him. "You bottom for him?"

"I'm trying to figure out why the hell you would care if I did."

"Guess I have my answer. And you know why."

"Not anymore, Styx. Too much time's passed."

He felt Styx's body stiffen, thought the man would release him. And then...

And then Styx's hand went to his cock as he sucked on the back of Law's neck along the spot—*that spot*—he'd discovered drove Law wild.

The only one who'd ever found it and oh God, he was going to come in his fucking pants if Styx didn't stop.

And Styx *would not stop*.

"Like that, baby?" Styx whispered after licking the spot where Law knew there'd be a red mark that would stay there for days, then used his tongue and teeth and hands, slipped into Law's half unzipped jeans to work his magic.

"Fuck...please...don't, Styx." But he was saying don't and meant, *don't stop*. And it was something he wanted—needed—too much to struggle more.

He'd always been a goddamned whore for this man—that would never change.

"Styx." The name, moaned into the dark, and if the man called him by his nickname, he'd lose it in his pants.

A few minutes and then a husky whisper answered, "Yeah, come right now, Law."

LC had no choice. His body always deferred to Styx's wishes. *Always.*

ABOUT THE AUTHOR

Stephanie Tyler is the *New York Times* bestselling author of romance novels spanning multiple genres, including Romantic Suspense, New Adult, Paranormal Romance and Contemporary Romance. She's a hybrid author who writes for multiple publishers, including Random House, NAL/Penguin, Harlequin, Carina Press, Mammoth Books, Belle Books and Samhain Publishing, as well as Riptide (as SE Jakes) and indie publishing. Her books have been translated into half a dozen languages, nominated for an RT Readers' Choice Award and garnered top picks from *RT Books Magazine* as well as starred reviews from *Publishers Weekly*. She's a frequent workshop presenter and has contributed stories for anthologies for charities, including **SEAL of My Dreams**, which has raised over 150K for the Veterans Medical Association.

Visit Stephanie Tyler at www.stephanietyler.com.

***

SE Jakes is the pen name for *New York Times* bestselling author Stephanie Tyler, and half the co-writing team of Sydney Croft. First published in 2011, SE Jakes has quickly risen to be a bestselling author in the LGBT romance genre, as well as a fan favorite. Her books are frequently highlighted in *USA Today* and have been reviewed by *Library Journal* and *RT Books Maga-*

zine. She's been nominated by several sites for Favorite M/M author and has finaled in the Goodreads M/M Romance Readers Choice Awards in 7 categories. She's a hybrid author who writes for Riptide Publishing and Samhain Publishing, and she indie publishes as well.

Visit SE Jakes at www.sejakes.com.

Sydney Croft is the alter ego of Stephanie Tyler and Larissa Ione, two *New York Times* bestselling authors who blend their very different writing interests into adventurous tales of erotic paranormal fiction. Together, they developed a world where people with extraordinary abilities, like the power to control storms, could live and work with others like them. The series has been described as "Erotica meets the X-Men," and is unique in its own "erotic superhero romance" niche. Larissa and Stephanie live in different states and communicate almost entirely through email, though they often get together for conferences and book signings.

Visit Sydney Croft at www.sydneycroft.com.

For more information:
www.sejakes.com
authorsejakes@gmail.com

ALSO BY SE JAKES

Men of Honor Series

Bound By Honor

Bound By Law

Ties That Bind

Bound By Danger

Bound For Keeps

Bound To Break

———

Phoenix, Inc. Series

No Boundaries

———

Inked Series

Hold The Line

Thirds

———

EE LTD. Universe

Free Falling

Hell or High Water Series

Catch A Ghost

Long Time Gone

Daylight Again

Not Fade Away

If I Ever

Dirty Deeds Series

Dirty Deeds

Havoc MC Series

Running Wild

Running Blind

Bluewater Bay (multi-author series)

No Easy Way (novella)

in the *Lights, Camera, Action* Anthology

WRITING AS STEPHANIE TYLER

Shelter Series

Shelter Me

Pieces of Me (*forthcoming*)

Mirror Series

Mirror Me

Rule Of Thirds

Walk In My Shadow

Double Blind (coming soon)

Skulls Creek MC Series

Vipers Run

Vipers Rule

Section 8 Series

Surrender

Unbreakable

Fragmented

Defiance Series

Defiance

Redemption

Salvation

The Defiance Series Collection

(Defiance, Redemption & Salvation)

Temperance

Dire Wolves Series

Dire Warning (prequel novella)

Dire Needs

Dire Wants

Dire Desires

Shadow Force Series

Lie With Me

Promises In The Dark

In The Air Tonight

Night Moves

Lonely Is The Night

Hold Series

Hard To Hold

Too Hot To Hold

Hold On Tight

Holding On (novella)

Hot Nights, Dark Desires Anthology

Night Vision (novella)

Harlequin Blaze

Coming Undone

Risking It All

Beyond His Control

WRITING AS SYDNEY CROFT

ACRO Series

Riding The Storm

Unleashing The Storm

Seduced By The Storm

Taming The Fire

Tempting The Fire

Taken By Fire

Three The Hard Way (novella)

Hot Nights, Dark Desires Anthology

Shadow Play (novella)